Night of the Wild Stags

A Reverse Harem Shifter Romance

By Golden Angel

© 2018 Golden Angel LLC

Acknowledgements

I have a lot of people to thank for helping me with this book.

Marie for all her help with catching small errors and the continuity issues I occasionally struggle with (I swear, she remembers all the things that I can't). Karen for catching my lack of commas and commas in the wrong places, mixed-up words, and my overuse of certain words and phrases. Katherine, for her ever-lasting support, encouragement and suggestions. Michelle for her comments, questions, and suppositions, which always end up changing the way the plot and character development flows. Sir Nick for providing the much-needed male perspective, requests for clarification when my writing is confusing, and making me aware of continuity issues.

Lee Savino for being my author-sensei.

Miranda for her quick editing skills, words of support, and general awesomeness.

My husband for his continued loved and support.

And, as always, a big thank you to all of you for buying and reading my work... if you love it, please leave a review!

Table of Contents

Chapter 1 4

Chapter 2 18

Chapter 3 32

Chapter 4 46

Chapter 5 61

Chapter 6 75

Chapter 7 90

Chapter 8 102

Chapter 9 117

Epilogue 131

About the Author 135

Chapter 1

The knowledge of her inevitable doom crept up Kiara's spine as she forced one foot in front of the other, shivering despite the warm afternoon. She'd been walking for miles down this road without seeing another living creature. There were a few in the woods, she could smell them, but they were all regular animals.

Not other shifters. Not even humans.

No help.

Dismay rose up inside of her, choking her with the unfairness of it all.

A few months of freedom, a few months of glorious independence and autonomy, of making her own choices and living her own life... had the elders been right? Was this the price she would pay for leaving the herd?

No.

No dammit.

Kiara hadn't given in to their warnings. She hadn't given in to the mating she hadn't chosen. She hadn't given in to being smacked around for the rest of her life.

If she died here and now of this sickness, it would be because of biology and chance. It wasn't a punishment or a judgment, even if she knew the elders would claim it was.

But she didn't want to die. She wanted to live.

She could barely feel her animal anymore, but she felt the tiniest bit of agreement pushing through from the back of her mind.

Neither of them were ready to give up.

So even as her body was wracked with spasms, even as she dry-heaved every ten feet or so, she kept forcing one foot in front of the other. Only one thought was on her mind: her destination.

Lakewood.

******

"Ahhh... vacation..."

Dorian glanced in the rearview mirror of the car to see his cousin Alec spreading out his arms and legs so that he nearly took up two seats just by himself. Alec's older brother Riley, who was sitting next to him, glanced up from the tablet he was reading on and gave Alec a pointed a look. Unperturbed, Alec just grinned and made sure he wasn't *quite* touching Riley's space.

"What do you all want to do when we get to the cabin?" Gavin, Dorian's twin asked. He was sitting beside Dorian in the front seat of the car and he looked just as excited as Alec. "I think I might just nap for the whole first day."

"Not until we're done unpacking," Dorian said sternly.

Even though he was only three minutes older than Gavin, that still made him the oldest of their herd of four and he usually took the unofficial 'alpha' position. Since they were soldiers at Lakewood and technically considered part of Eli Mansfield's pack they didn't actually have need for a real herd alpha, but when they were on their own for a few days (or a week, like now) Dorian always found himself assuming the role. None of the others seemed to mind. Hell, Alec encouraged it, preferring to have less responsibility, especially when they weren't at the Lakewood compound.

The four of them looked alike, but they were all very different.

Dorian and Gavin were nearly identical twins. Gavin's hair was a shade lighter than Dorian's, which was nearly impossible to decipher unless they were standing right next to each other. Dorian had finally grown a goatee just to help differentiate them. Gavin was definitely a prankster though, he and Alec were often pulling practical jokes—mostly on each other, fortunately—whereas Dorian thought the two were idiots for wasting their time on the elaborate setups which had no real effect on their lives.

He and Riley spent more time together, tending to pair off while their younger brothers ran wild. Riley and Alec both had dark hair like Gavin and Dorian, but Riley's eyes were hazel green and Alec's were more amber than hazel. Alec also often had stubble on his face, although he never grew out his facial hair like Dorian did. He was just too lazy to shave most days.

"Unpack?" Alec snorted his derision. "I'm just going to go naked or stag the whole time we're there. I don't need to unpack."

All of them were red deer shifters and they were very much looking forward to spending some serious time in their other forms. They didn't *need* to constantly take stag form in order to placate their inner animals, but they all enjoyed being out in nature as their animals, and indulged whenever possible. Inside Dorian's head, he could feel his own stag lifting his majestically antlered head in anticipation.

"Then what's in that big bag taking up half the trunk?" Riley asked, looking annoyed at his younger brother. Dorian had to admit, he was curious too.

"Carefully wrapped booze bottles, a box of cigars, and some magazines," Alec said carelessly.

Dorian shook his head. He was sure there were probably some clothes in there as well—cushioning the glass bottles probably—but it would be just like Alec to pack the bare minimum for human living. The magazines were probably either naked chicks or barely clothed chicks on motorcycles and hot rods.

"Dude, I don't want to be staring at your junk all week," Gavin said, groaning with disgust. "We're going to be on vacation. How am I supposed to enjoy myself if I'm constantly swamped with pity for you?"

"Hey, my junk is amazing," Alec said, sitting up straight and reaching down between his legs to cup the equipment in question. "It's bigger than yours."

"It sure as hell is not."

Sometimes Gavin and Alec seemed more like brothers than cousins, Dorian reflected, wondering if he was about to have to take the fatherly position.

"You're just jealous because Sheila didn't want to get down and dirty with you."

"That's enough," Dorian said sternly, deciding to head the argument off early. Mostly because he couldn't take five more minutes of this crap from them, much less twenty.

"What are you going to do, pull the car over?" Alec asked, jeering. "Hey... wait... seriously?"

"Shut up, this isn't about you." Dorian put the car in park, only slightly amused at the timing, and peered into the rearview mirror. Not at his cousins, but out the back at the splash of white and brown on the side of the road. He'd thought he'd seen the pile of cloth moving as they'd driven past it, but maybe it had just been the wind—no, there it went again. That wasn't just fabric, there was something alive and moving. "I'll be right back."

******

As Dorian got out of the car and started walking back along the road, Riley twisted in his seat, frowning as he watched his cousin walk back down the road. Dorian's behavior was extremely unusual, to say the least. His strides were purposeful, quick.

"What is he doing?" Riley murmured.

"There's something back there," Alec said, not even opening his eyes. He looked like he was on the verge of falling asleep right there. "You know how cautious Dorian is, he probably just wants to check it out."

"I'm going to see what it is," Riley said. He was disturbed by Dorian's unanticipated actions and he hated being cooped up in a small space anyway. Even though the sedan was plenty spacious, all four of them were big guys and being in the back meant less leg space than the front. Inside his head, his stag was urging him to get out of the car. Both of them preferred more open spaces.

Neither his brother nor his cousin responded, which he took to mean they didn't care what he did. He undid his seatbelt and hopped out of the car. Closing the door behind him, he stretched his arms up towards the sky and then dropped them down. Dorian was nearing what looked like a small pile of old clothes on the side of the road, about fifty yards back.

Shrugging his muscles loose, Riley did a little half jog to catch up. He'd rather see what had caught Dorian's interest than hang around the car.

Dorian's sudden tension alerted him that something was wrong as his older cousin circled around the small pile, and Riley picked up his pace, his stag lifting up its head and looking for danger. Coming closer, it became clear the bundle wasn't just a pile of clothing—there was a *woman* wearing the pile. There was way too much clothing for such a warm day, but she appeared to be shivering.

"Is she hurt?" Riley asked, coming up behind Dorian then passing him and dropping to his knees, his hand going to the female's forehead.

"Riley, wait!" Dorian reached out his own hand to stop him, but it was too late. He heard the aggravated noise Dorian made but ignored it.

"She's burning up!" Riley said, concern shooting through him.

The woman was very petite, slender, and her pale, nearly white hair had been pulled back into a braid. He smelled chemicals around her head, which likely meant the color was dyed—especially taking into account her dark eyebrows. Although there was a fair amount of dirt on her face, her delicate bone structure made her look almost ethereally beautiful underneath the grime.

Beneath the chemicals used on her hair and the odor of sweat and unwashed flesh, he could also smell her animal. She was a shifter. Some kind of doe, although her scent was a little different than any other doe he'd met before. His stag wanted to take a deeper whiff, ignoring the rest of her smell, curious about the peculiarity of her scent.

"Dammit, Riley, you don't know what's wrong with her," Dorian said, scolding him. "What if she's contagious? Look at her hands, look at the spots!"

"Spots?" Riley frowned, lifting up her hand to examine it more closely. Yes, just as Dorian said, she had lesions on her skin. He hadn't been able to initially see them under the grime on her skin. "That makes no sense. She smells like a deer, she can't..."

His voice trailed off and then both he and Dorian looked at each other, alarm in both of their expressions.

The only disease which effected shifters and also caused symptoms like this was the Scourge. But the Scourge was not a disease which caused this kind of reaction in adults. It was a childhood illness which they all grew out of. Riley hadn't heard of a single large shifter adult having the Scourge, ever. The only adult shifters it ever effected were small animal shifters.

There were quite a few diseases which ravaged the smaller shifter population, making many of them extinct, but which barely effected larger shifters other than as bad colds. With smaller shifters the Scourge caused extreme nausea and vomiting. The victims couldn't keep down any food and ended up slowly starving to death as they wilted away with fever. The slightly blueish spots covering her were impossible, and yet there was no denying the evidence of his eyes.

"A mutated variation of the Scourge?" he said, his voice lilting up to make the statement a rhetorical question. Obviously Dorian wouldn't know any better than he did, although they could hypothesize. His tone turned grim. "Perhaps large shifters are no longer immune."

In which case, they were all in danger.

"I've already touched her," Riley said, his voice hardening. He looked up at Dorian. "You should stay back. If it's airborne you might already be contaminated, but if it's not..." His voice choked slightly.

They both stared at each other.

Riley was uncertain how long they might have stood there, staring at each other in silence, both of them trying to decide exactly how to proceed next, if it wasn't for their impulsive and immature younger brothers.

He saw the stags jumping out of the forest behind Dorian, and his eyes went wide, but before he could even begin to shout a warning to stay back, both were jumping forward in an attempt to startle Dorian.

It was a game they often played, but they'd never succeeded.

They did today.

Alec's shoulder bumped into Dorian from behind, sending his cousin sprawling. Jumping up, Riley managed to catch Dorian before he fell on the woman—but any hopes of keeping the other two from being exposed to whatever contagion the woman was carrying had just died. Gavin was already sniffing at her hair, his buck obviously both interested and confused.

"You *fucking idiots!*" Dorian roared as he straightened up, face red with both fear and fury. "Stay back!"

"It's too late now," Riley said pragmatically, sighing, even as he felt the same fear. Alec had already shifted and was touching the female's leg, crouching naked beside her, his face concerned.

"What's wrong with her?" Alec asked.

"We think it's the Scourge," Riley said, causing Gavin's stag to jump back. Too late. Obviously Gavin understood the implications, although Alec didn't immediately.

"But that's impossible," Alec said, still frowning as a grim-faced and silent Dorian scooped the woman up into his arms.

"Apparently not," Dorian said. He turned and started back to the car, the woman cradled in his arms. "We have to go back to Lakewood. Call it in, Riley, and let them know what's coming."

******

Her doe prodded her, rousing her.

Someone was holding her. Loud voices. Warmth. People.

Hope.

Lakewood.

"Lakewood."

"What was that, sweetheart?" A male voice in her ear. Deep. Soothing in a rumbling way. She didn't recognize it. Probably not Sebastian or anyone from home then. She knew all of their voices.

"Lakewood," she begged, her mouth was so dry she could barely rasp the word.

"She's asking to go to Lakewood," the man said, more loudly. Speaking to the others who were there.

Lakewood.

Hope.

Please... let me live.

******

Well this wasn't how he'd expected his vacation to go. Twenty minutes into the drive and they were already turning back around to Lakewood, this time with an extra passenger. A possibly contagious one carrying a possibly deadly disease.

Not a very nice death either, if there was such a thing.

Still, if Alec had to choose how he was going to die, vomiting to death was not high on his list of preferences. It sounded fucking awful.

Too late though. He and Gavin had decided to try and sneak up on Dorian, give him a scare—something they'd never managed before.

Well his older cousin was plenty scared now.

Alec looked down at the shivering female deer shifter resting her head on his thigh. Her feet were on Riley's and he wasn't sure who had gotten the better end of the deal. She did look like she might clean up nicely but she obviously hadn't bathed recently and they had to keep the windows closed because of her possible contagion, which didn't help.

Alec's stag was much more interested in their unexpected passenger than Alec would have expected. Normally his stag couldn't care less what female Alec occupied his time with. Why the animal was so interested in this one, he had no idea.

"Why do you think she was on foot?" he asked, glancing at Riley's lap where he could see her well-worn sneakers. They had definitely seen better days.

"That's a good question," Dorian said grimly, his hands tightening around the steering wheel, making the leather squeak a little. Yeah, he was still pissed.

"I guess she must not have a car," Riley said, looking down at her with an odd expression on his face. He'd been acting a bit odd since they'd found her actually. Like he was drawn to her.

She tugged at Alec's heartstrings too. How could she not? She was obviously suffering but strong enough to have made it all the way from regular civilization halfway down the long road to Lakewood on foot. He admired her strength, even as he worried over the lightness of her weight. Was it normal to feel so protective so quickly? His stag didn't seem bothered by it. If anything both of his sides felt unusually intrigued by her.

As a soldier, Alec had protected many people—men, women, and children, but he'd never had quite this reaction before. There was just something about her. He spent the rest of the drive back to Lakewood worrying over both her and his brother and cousins.

A little bit himself too. He really didn't want to die by vomit.

Riley had called ahead to the compound and let them know what was happening, so when they arrived the guards recognized their car and waved them through the entrance. More than one peered curiously through the windows but didn't attempt to get too close to the car. Dorian pulled around to the side entrance of the hospital where several people dressed in hazmat suits were already waiting for them.

Riley carried the female in his arms, placing her on the gurney provided. Alec felt a strange surge of jealousy over Riley being the one to do so, which made no sense at all. He didn't know the woman, and she smelled kinda bad. So why was he wishing he'd been the one to carry her?

They were led to a quarantine room where they were met with two more doctors in hazmat suits and all four men were put through a rigorous cleansing and decontamination procedure. Fresh clothes were left out for them in the room they weren't supposed to leave.

Sighing, Alec wandered over to the window and looked outside. In the distance he could see the woods. Surprisingly, his stag was way more interested in where the female had been taken than in staring at the woods they were all supposed to be running through right now.

"Well," said Gavin when they were finally all done and sitting in the plastic chairs. "Some start to our vacation this is."

His twin glared at him. "If two idiots hadn't—"

"We'd still be here, dumbass," Gavin shot back. "You really think Alec and I would have just gone on vacation while you were back here in quarantine?"

Well that was true enough.

******

Finally having agreed to disagree, Gavin and Dorian sat back in their chairs.

Which, unfortunately, left Gavin with very little to do. He looked around the room. Riley and Alec were both staring off into space with very similar expressions, although he doubted they were thinking about anything similar. The two brothers were basically polar opposites.

A little like him and Dorian he supposed, eyeing his twin. Although that was partly because Dorian tended to take everything way too seriously in Gavin's opinion. Sometimes it was needed, but Gavin considered it his job to be Dorian's right-hand man in a number of ways. Supporting him when he was acting as their herd's alpha but also making sure Dorian actually let loose and had some fun now and then. It was something he needed in both human and stag form.

The door to the quarantine room suddenly opened and they all turned as one. Gavin and Dorian jumping to their feet in concern and confusion when they saw Dr. Tran in her regular clothing without a hazmat suit.

"You're all clear," she said briskly, her eyes taking in each one of them in turn. Despite her diminutive size, the doctor was never intimidated no matter how large the soldiers towering over her were. Knowing she could turn into a four hundred pound tiger at any given moment probably helped. "She *does* have the Scourge—"

"How?" Alec interrupted her, bewildered. Dr. Tran gave him a pointed look.

"I bet if you're quiet, she'll tell us," Riley muttered, and Gavin saw Dorian's lips twitch. He'd be willing to bet his twin had been about to say the same thing.

"After we got an IV in her and began to re-hydrate her, she woke up enough to tell us she's a Pudu deer shifter," Dr. Tran explained.

Her explanation didn't make anything clearer to Gavin. "What's a Pudu deer?"

"They're the smallest deer in the world," she said. "Think, the size of a lamb when fully grown."

All of the men made various noises of understanding. So she was both a deer and a small shifter, which explained why the Scourge was affecting her so badly. Killing her, actually. They didn't need to worry about the Scourge because the doctors had actually recently been able to come up with a vaccine for the larger shifters. So far no one had been able to test it on smaller shifters.

Gavin frowned. Even though he didn't know her, he didn't like the idea of her dying, especially not after she'd come so far. His stag made a distressed noise, unhappy at the idea as well. Something about her had called to his animal and it had apparently become more attached than he'd realized.

"Are you going to be able to help her?" Dorian asked, his thoughts obviously working along the same lines. In fact, all of them were earnestly focused on Dr. Tran, waiting for her verdict.

"We're testing her DNA right now to see if she fits the parameters for our only known cure," Dr. Tran said carefully, making all four males snort. They knew exactly what she was talking about. It was the worst-kept secret at Lakewood.

"We know the Bunsons," Riley said. "We basically know how it works." The three Bunson brothers had all trained at Lakewood and pretty much everyone knew they were hybrid shifters, originally fully human, who were created in a lab by a mad

15

scientist trying to find ways to prevent smaller shifters from dying out. Unfortunately, his ethics had left a lot to be desired.

Now Dr. Montgomery was in the basement in a well-guarded cell beneath the hospital of Lakewood, still continuing some of his work. He'd kept so much of it in his head, it was impossible to replicate any of it without him. His work was also how they'd managed to come up with a vaccine, from what Gavin knew.

The Bunsons were going without justice, but at the same time, their sacrifice was making it possible for lives to be saved. Rumor had it a couple of squirrels had been the most recent beneficiaries of Dr. Montgomery's work, and one of them had actually mated one of the Bunsons. Riley had been fascinated by the tale. Gavin hadn't cared so much other than knowing who the enemy was. Dr. Montgomery worked for an entity called The Company and they'd attacked Lakewood as well as a shifter stronghold, trying to recover both the doctor and their escaped test subjects.

As far as Gavin understood it, if she didn't have some kind of larger shifter in her ancestry, she was pretty much fucked. Dr. Montgomery's cure wasn't actually a cure, he changed a person's DNA, creating a hybrid of the original shifter with a larger shifter, using their recessive genes. The problem was that a lot of smaller shifter communities had been very insular, rarely mating outside of their species, which meant even Dr. Montgomery's 'cure' wouldn't always work.

"Thank you all for bringing her in," Dr. Tran said. "You're free to go, the quarantine isn't necessary."

And with that, she left the room.

They all looked at each other.

As eager as Gavin had been to go and just sleep for a while, he wasn't sure that was what he wanted to do now. His buck definitely didn't. The animal was pacing back and forth in his head, restless, but not for the outdoors... it wanted to check on the doe. So did Gavin. Just to see how she was. It only seemed polite.

Dorian cleared his throat, ready to lead the way as usual. "I'd like to check on the woman on our way out, if that's okay with the rest of you."

"Yup."

"Fine by me."

"Lead the way," Gavin said, adding his agreement behind Alec and Riley's.

Seemed like they were all on the same page. The excited clatter of metaphorical hooves in his head confirmed it.

Chapter 2

When Kiara woke up she felt normal. Tired, achy, but normal.

Which was unexpected. She'd thought she'd wake up feeling different. Abnormal even. After all, she'd signed off on having her actual DNA changed in order to save her life.

At least she didn't feel sick anymore either. No more shivering, no more creeping cold on a warm day, no more nausea that twisted her insides and made her want to vomit. She was definitely okay with feeling back to normal, she was just surprised by it.

She prodded her doe in her head. The shy animal gave her a metaphorical nuzzle back, much more awake and aware than she had been in days, but still giving off a sleepy vibe. Which was understandable. Kiara was still feeling pretty sleepy too.

So what had woken her?

Opening her eyes, she was rather startled to see she wasn't alone in the hospital room—there were four men she'd never seen before all lined up, fast asleep in chairs along the wall opposite her bed. Four very large, very handsome men. Her doe perked up a little bit as she took in the sight of their dark heads and similar, equally attractive, features.

Movement out of the corner of her eye had her turning her head to see who was there. A blonde woman in green scrubs was fiddling with something in a drawer. It must have been her coming in, or maybe opening the drawer, which had woken Kiara.

She looked over and met Kiara's gaze, her own blue eyes widening with delight to see Kiara awake. Putting her finger to her lips to indicate Kiara should be quiet, the nurse glanced over at the line of men, before coming closer to Kiara. Her blue eyes danced with amusement as she took in Kiara's confusion.

"How are you feeling?" the nurse whispered, glancing at the monitors connected to Kiara's body, reading her pulse and other things... Kiara didn't know, she had no medical training.

"Tired, but okay," she whispered back. She looked over at the line of men. "Who are they?"

"Your rescuers. They've been here since they brought you in two days ago." The nurse's blue eyes glinted with excitement, confusing Kiara further. Seeing the expression on Kiara's face, the nurse just chuckled, shaking her head. "Not a romantic, huh?"

She used to be, but maybe not so much anymore. Kiara peered at the men. They were all gorgeous and she was extremely grateful, but she still didn't understand why they were there. They might have rescued her—she remembered a lot of deep, male voices and someone carrying her before she woke up long enough to tell the doctor what was wrong—but she didn't actually know them.

"I'm going to go get Dr. Tran," the nurse said, patting Kiara's arm. "She'll want to examine you now that you're awake." Slipping out of the room, the nurse closed the door behind her.

Kiara was still sleepy, but she was determined to remain awake.

After all, there were four strange men in her room. Big men. Although, the nurse hadn't seemed to find anything unusual about that. And they had rescued her.

Maybe they weren't dangerous to her. But she still couldn't relax enough to completely let her guard down, no matter how safe the nurse obviously felt she was.

Since she was all alone and none of them were looking at her, she took the opportunity to study them. Her doe was interested too, still just as sleepy as she was, but also curious about the strange males.

They all looked related. Similar facial features, although one of them had a goatee and another was pretty scruffy around the jawline. The scruffiest one also had the longest hair. The other two were clean shaven, but one of them looked a *lot* like the one with a goatee while the other looked more like Scruffy.

To her surprise and horror, she found her body responding to their presence—her skin tingling a little bit, butterflies beginning to flap in her stomach as a blush worked its way up her cheeks the longer she looked at them. Her blush turned even hotter when the diminutive doctor she remembered from before opened the door and stepped quietly inside.

"You're looking much better," Dr. Tran said approvingly, but quietly, as she neared Kiara's bed, looking her over. She held out her hand and Kiara lifted her own so the doctor could inspect her arm. "No more lesions, good."

"I don't feel any different," Kiara whispered. "I mean, I feel better and I don't feel sick anymore but... shouldn't my doe feel different?" After all, supposedly her genes had been changed so she was a Pudu deer-jaguar hybrid now. Apparently some distant ancestor had gotten freaky with a jaguar shifter, which Kiara had trouble imagining considering how restrictive and isolationist her community was.

The doctor hesitated and gave her a rather rueful smile. "Unfortunately I'm not the best person to ask about that, but I do know there will be some people present in the compound this afternoon who will be able to answer your questions about being changed the way you have been."

Others who had been changed, like her? Kiara was instantly curious.

"That would be great, thank you," she said, relief suffusing her voice.

She didn't think she'd whispered any louder than they had been, but sudden movement across the room caught her attention. Scruffy was yawning and stretching, obviously waking up. He was even cuter with his eyes open, as much as Kiara tried not to notice. As soon as he saw her, his hazel eyes lit up.

"You're awake," he said gleefully. Unlike Kiara and Dr. Tran, he didn't bother to keep his voice down and the other men next to him immediately jerked to life as well.

Kiara felt something deep inside of her stir—not her doe, but more like a feeling or a sensation... a craving she'd never felt before—as she watched them. Just like Scruffy, they all became even more attractive as their personalities animated their faces. In contrast, Kiara felt about as attractive as a toadstool. Someone had given her a sponge bath so she wasn't as disgusting as she remembered being when she'd first been brought to the hospital, but she wasn't exactly feeling fresh either. She was also suddenly acutely aware of a dire need to brush her teeth.

"How are you feeling?" Scruffy asked, bounding up to stand beside her bed before the other men had even fully woken. Her eyes widened in slight alarm at his exuberant approach, but Dr. Tran just smiled at him.

"Um, I'm okay, thank you," Kiara said shyly, nervously plucking at the sheet covering her and feeling increasingly vulnerable as all the men stood and came closer. They were all grinning at her as they surrounded her bed, which just made her feel even more awkward. The only reason she wasn't totally freaking out was Dr. Tran's presence. The doctor didn't seem the slightest bit intimidated by the large men dwarfing her.

"You look a lot better," Scruffy said, surprising her by taking her hand. "You smell better too."

As Kiara stifled a giggle, her nerves subsiding a little at his gentle touch and frank words, the man standing on the other side of him slapped the back of his head.

"Dude! Who taught you how to talk to women?"

"You," Scruffy said pointedly, not even wincing at the rough slap. He winked at Kiara as the other man gasped in mock outrage. Their silliness was actually calming her more than anything else they could have done.

"I sure as hell did not." The man leaned forward, giving Kiara an earnest look. "I swear, I did not teach him to talk to women that way."

"Would the two of you shut up?" Goatee said, managing to sound resigned, disgusted, and very slightly amused all at once. The man standing next to him blinked at her, making her label him in her head as the quiet one. Goatee seemed kind of like a leader and the man next to Scruffy... was definitely a charmer. Scruffy was the silly one, although he was also charming in his silliness. Goatee fixed his dark gaze on Kiara, making her want to squirm under the heavy weight of his attention. He didn't scare her though; if anything his gentle gaze made her feel almost protected. "Hi. We're really glad to see you looking better."

"If you didn't know, these are the gentlemen who found you and brought you in," Dr. Tran said with an amused smile as she scooted around the bed to give herself more space, before picking up the chart at the foot of it and marking something off with her pen. "I'll leave you all to get acquainted while I go make a call and see if I can't arrange that visit I mentioned. Rest for a bit and when I come back I'd like to examine your animal."

Giving Kiara a reassuring smile, the doctor left the room. There seemed to be an assumption by both the nurse and the doctor that all four men were safe and Kiara should feel comfortable with them.

Strangely enough, she did... but that just made her worried as well. Why on earth did she feel so comfortable with four strangers? Even her doe wasn't doing more than sleepily observing them, and her animal was skittish at the best of times. Especially after leaving her community.

"Hi," she said, tugging her hand away from Scruffy's, because she was starting to feel weird about holding it for so long. "Um, I'm Kiara Arrio."

As she'd hoped, introducing herself immediately prodded them into giving their own names. Goatee was Dorian Walker, Scruffy was Alec Walker, the charmer was Gavin Walker, and the quiet one finally spoke up to say his name was Riley Walker.

"And um, you are all related?" she asked, unable to think of anything else to say, despite the obvious answer to her question.

"These two are twins," Alec said, gesturing to Dorian and Gavin. "Riley's my older brother, and we're all cousins." Well, that explained that.

Chewing the inside of her lip, Kiara tried to think of something else to say.

"Is there anyone you need us to call?" Dorian asked, his dark eyes steadily focused on her face, making her feel as though he was examining every minute change in her expression. Out of all of them, he definitely made her feel the most nervous, but at the same time she also had the odd notion of being protected by his presence. "You were all alone when we found you but we weren't sure..."

He cut off as Kiara shook her head frantically, slight panic welling up inside of her.

******

"No, no one," the pretty female said, her eyes growing wide and upset at the notion.

"Shh, it's okay," Alec said, taking her hand again. Dorian felt a little spurt of jealousy at how easily Alec just reached out and touched her—and how easily she accepted it. She obviously found him charming, whereas she seemed a little intimidated by Dorian. Which wasn't unusual, most people were and normally it didn't bother him, but right now he wished he was more of a people person like Alec or Gavin.

"Are you in trouble?" Riley asked, moving closer and sounding concerned. "Can we help?"

The other three all exchanged surprised glances as Kiara focused on Riley, her hand still in Alec's. In a lot of ways Riley was even less social than Dorian. He'd been so quiet since they'd picked up their little lost waif that hearing him offering to jump in and help now was unexpected. None of them looked like they wanted to disagree though.

Dorian definitely didn't.

Something about the pretty doe called to him, and had ever since he'd found her in a crumpled heap on the side of the road. He didn't seem to be alone in that either. None of them had wanted to leave her side while she recovered. In fact, he was pretty sure if he'd tried, his stag wouldn't have let him.

The feeling of firm agreement drifted up from the back of his mind, making Dorian's lips curve into a smile.

Kiara looked around at all of them, looking even smaller and more vulnerable than she had a moment ago. Her gaze dropped to her lap. "I'm not in trouble. There's nothing... I'm fine. As soon as I'm better I'll be on my way. You don't need to worry about me."

This time all four of them exchanged glances, as Riley looked up as well. Yeah, she was a terrible liar. Why and about what he didn't know, but obviously she was in trouble. His buck lifted his head, wicked antlers at the ready, but there was no one to fight at the moment.

Unfortunately they didn't get the opportunity to talk with her more about it, because Dr. Tran came back in the room and kicked them all out. She needed to examine Kiara's animal, for which she wanted privacy.

As soon as they were in the hall, Dorian felt restless and uneasy. His buck didn't like being separated from Kiara. He wasn't a big fan of it either, to be honest. Over the past two days he'd kinda gotten used to hanging around her room with his brother and cousins, waiting for her to wake up. Which... was kinda creepy when he thought too much about it, but they weren't trying to be creepy, they just wanted to make sure she was okay.

He had been trying to convince himself it was just because, as the ones who found her, they all felt responsible, but he was starting to think it was a little bit more than that.

"So... is anyone else feeling oddly really attached to Miss Kiara?" Gavin asked, shoving his hands in his pockets and hunching his shoulders slightly, as if he was afraid everyone was going to deny their pretty obvious feelings.

"Yup," Alec said, giving the closed door a look of longing, which was pretty out of character. Alec loved women—plural. He wasn't really the type to pine after any particular one. Yet, somehow Dorian wasn't surprised. This particular woman seemed to have definitely gotten under their skin.

"Do you think it's the mating phenomenon?" Riley asked, tilting his head to the side and staring off at nothing in particular, as he often did when considering a question.

Alec pinched the bridge of his nose, taking in a deep breath and sighing. "Can you just call it mating, please? Or hooking up? Screwing? Anything but mating phenomenon?"

"I just think it's possible something about Kiara has triggered our call to mate," Riley said haughtily. "Maybe there's a pheromone in her olfactory makeup or—"

"Aaaaah! Stop," Alec whined, putting his hands over his ears and making his older brother grin. Since Alec's head was down, he couldn't see Riley's expression.

Someday Alec would realize when his brother was trolling him, but it apparently wasn't going to be today.

Ignoring both of them, Dorian cleared his throat. "I'd like to stay here and help her. Instead of going on vacation."

He wasn't too surprised when they all immediately agreed.

******

Kiara asked for privacy to rest after Dr. Tran finished examining her doe. She was exhausted after shifting twice and it was a lot to absorb.

Although her doe didn't feel any different in her head, the little animal now weighed nearly a third more than she used to, had put on twice the amount of muscle she'd had before, and sported a mouth full of very sharp teeth. Once she'd changed, she'd also discovered she had a newly found craving for red meat. Once she'd shifted back to human, she'd asked for a large steak. Rare.

The deep rumble of voices in the hallway outside her room indicated the four stags who had rescued her hadn't gone anywhere. She didn't know what to think about that. Part of her was thrilled they were still there, another part of her was wary.

Her doe came down on the thrilled side. The animal didn't see them as a threat at all. In fact, her doe seemed a little cocky now, but Kiara supposed she couldn't blame her. After all, she'd gone from being very easy prey whose best defense was hiding, to becoming a predator.

But why were the men still there? The question niggled at her as she finally fell back asleep.

Several hours later, she woke up again when the door to her room opened. Immediately, Kiara came alert, her doe searching for the threat and ready to take it out. The first reaction was familiar, the second definitely was not.

"Hi Kiara," Dr. Tran said, smiling as she came into the room. Behind her was a woman with auburn hair and friendly grey eyes, smiling at her in a sympathetic and understanding manner. "This is Jesse O'Neal—sorry, Bunson, she's mated now. Jesse was here not too long ago as well."

"Hi, it's nice to meet you," Jesse, the redhead, said cheerfully, grabbing a chair and pulling it over towards Kiara's bed. "So, I'm Jesse. I was a squirrel until I had the Torch and now I'm a squirrel-tiger hybrid."

Holy... Kiara knew about the Torch, although she'd never met anyone who had it, of course. Because the small shifter diseases were so devastating and—until recently—there was nothing that could be done about them, the sick were often quarantined. She'd heard the Torch felt like being burned alive from the inside out, there was nothing to do but give the victims morphine and try to keep them from feeling the debilitating pain until they finally passed. And Jesse had survived that!

"What's it like? Um... being, being both?" Kiara asked, fumbling over her words because she didn't really know how to phrase it. After all, they were talking about the impossible. Fortunately, Jesse seemed to know exactly what she meant.

"Well, for one, so far it seems to be a little different for males and females," Jesse said, her expression turning more serious as she leaned forward. "Are you about the same size you were before when you shift?" Kiara nodded. "Yeah, same for me and for one of the other females I know. My sister-in-law actually. I'm basically a squirrel with some serious claws and she's the Beast of Caerbannog... uh, Monty Python?" Jessie tried to explain when she saw the look of confusion on Kiara's face. But Kiara still had no idea what the other woman was talking about. "Aw, seriously? You poor thing, you're so sheltered."

Kiara smiled, because it was obvious Jesse was speaking lightly, teasing, but her smile felt a little brittle. Even though she'd been very sheltered, because of her job she'd figured out exactly how sheltered she was, and being on the run she'd proved it. There was an entire world she hadn't known about until she'd left the community. "You have no idea."

Apparently not realizing exactly how serious Kiara was, Jesse continued. "Well, she's basically a little murder bunny. Her older sister though, is the size of bear, as are all her brothers. And my brother, except since we're half-tiger he's really the size of a tiger, but basically it all makes for some very large, very weird looking bunnies and squirrels."

"And... you're... it's not..." Kiara sighed and wrinkled her nose. She was just going to have to be blunt. "No one is repulsed by this?"

Since she already wanted to be permanently finished with her old community and shifter society in general, she'd had no problem signing the form Dr. Tran had given her. It was just one more barrier against returning, she hoped. Although, considering how formidable her doe was now, even if

Sebastian wasn't completely repulsed by her new genetics, perhaps she could finally face him on more equal footing. Still, the idea that Jesse and these others she spoke of were completely accepted by all the other shifters around them was a bit shocking to her.

She'd expected to be shunned.

"Oh, I'm sure there are some," Jesse said, still cheerful. Her expression saddened for a moment. "My aunt refused the treatment and she wasn't approving of my brother and I having it done, but I like to think she understood in the end. We weren't ready to die yet. So far I haven't run into anyone bothered by it, mostly they're just incredibly nosy and want to see what my other half looks like. So get ready for all the questions." She rolled her eyes.

Kiara's own eyes widened. She wasn't expecting questions. She hadn't really been expecting anything at all from anyone. All she'd known was that there was a cure here at Lakewood. She hadn't known what the treatment actually was until Dr. Tran had explained why she had to sign a consent form to receive it.

Now all her assumptions were being turned on their head and she didn't quite know what to think.

Apparently regular shifter society was even more different than she'd anticipated.

"So, ah, speaking of questions," Jesse said, looking reluctant but like she was too curious not to ask. "There are four very attractive, very worried looking men just hanging out in the hallway outside your door... how come they aren't in here?"

"They..." Words were failing her again. But how could she explain what she didn't understand? "They rescued me, but for some reason they stayed afterwards... but I don't actually know them."

The look Jesse gave her now was full of amusement. "Do you want to know them?"

"What would I do with four males?" Kiara asked, completely confused—and even more so when Jesse coughed out a laugh.

"Ah, I can think of a few things, but I'm pretty sure my mate wouldn't approve."

Immediately, Kiara's shoulders hunched in on themselves as she tried to make herself smaller, a slight feeling of panic fluttering up in her. Her doe was caught between wanting to flee and looking around for something to fight. Of course, the second impulse was new. Kiara was much more used to fleeing.

"Kiara? Are you okay?" Jesse asked, reaching over to take Kiara's hand in much the same way Alec had.

"Will he be angry with you? Your mate?" Kiara asked softly, feeling a slight tremor go through her body. Jesse's eyes widened, her gaze sharpening as she stared at Kiara.

"No, my mate would certainly not be angry with me for any thoughts I had," Jesse said firmly. Her lips pressed into a flat line and then she pushed them into a smile before continuing. "I don't see a mating mark on your neck but... do you have a mate who hurt you?"

"A mating mark?" Kiara asked, honestly confused but also happy to avoid the question.

The other woman's sharp eyes weren't fooled but she still answered Kiara's question. "Like this."

There was what looked like the scar of a bite on her neck as she twisted her head, pulling down the collar of her shirt slowly to show Kiara. Fascinated despite herself, Kiara leaned forward. "Do all of his mates have one?"

"All of—?!" Jesse's words cut off and Kiara sat back, worried she'd overstepped her bounds somehow. "Kiara... Dr. Tran said you're a Pudu deer? I've never heard of that before. Maybe if you can tell me a bit about your mating rituals, I can tell you how my mating is different."

That made sense. After all, Kiara knew from reading that human mating rituals were different from her own community's. Her ever-present curiosity and the lack of threat she felt from Jesse spurred her forward.

"Well, Pudu deer are very solitary normally, but we've been forced to live in closer quarters than usual because our numbers are so small," she explained, her voice automatically taking on Sebastian's lecturing tone as she went over the information he so often used when instructing. "Pudu deer usually only meet to rut... my mate visits—*visited*—me on Wednesdays."

She kept her eyes downcast, not wanting Jesse to see how unhappy the arrangement had made her. After all, she should have been thrilled to have a mate at all. But while many of the females in her building had not seemed to mind, Kiara had longed for something more than a weekly visit from her mate. The Pudu herd had all lived together in the same building and the females were required to work so as not to create a burden on the few males. The advent of the internet had made the entire herd happy as they were able to work from their own places and not have to risk the various diseases killing other small shifters as they kept completely to themselves. Kiara had taken a job as a copy editor, which was where she'd read her first human romances and realized the kind of life she was longing for even before she knew it had existed, the unhappiness she hadn't been able to put into words.

Jesse's hand squeezed hers, but her voice remained calm and balanced. "Did your mate have other mates he was visiting on different days?"

Blinking back a tear, Kiara nodded her head, still keeping her gaze averted from Jesse's. She didn't know why she was so different from the other Pudu deer.

"I don't know why I was the only one unhappy," she confessed, the words spilling out under the gentle assault of Jesse's quiet, listening ear. No one had ever wanted to listen to her before. "Well, maybe not the only one, but most of them were content to just have their day with our mate... I read some human books though and what they described—one mate, just one, with emotion and touching outside of copulation, and... that's when I realized, that's what I wanted. So... I told him... I told him I no longer wanted to be his mate... He was so angry. He told me he'd kill me before he let me leave."

Kiara shuddered. He'd looked like he wanted to kill her too, the last time he'd found her. She'd hurt his standing with the others by running away, she knew she had.

"Kiara... Kiara, look at me, please," Jesse said, firmly but gently. Kiara lifted her gaze to the other woman's sympathetic, warm eyes. "That is *not* how mating is done here. I have heard something about deer herds before but... all parties in the mating must consent and want to be in it. There is always emotion, and touching, and intimacy, not just sex."

Listening fervently, Kiara gripped Jesse's hand back as the other woman told her everything she knew about shifter matings, and the little she'd heard about deer herds. Kiara didn't think she'd mind sharing so much if there had been more than just Sebastian's weekly visit to attempt a breeding, but there had never been any emotion there. No love.

And she hadn't been willing to live without it anymore.

Chapter 3

After Jesse left Kiara's room, leaving her rather shell-shocked about the vastly different world she'd been thrust into, the blonde nurse came in to ask if the Walkers could come back inside. Uncertain, but feeling bad that her rescuers were still hanging around outside, Kiara agreed.

She couldn't help but feel some trepidation, however. Jesse had confided she'd heard that red deer—the kind of deer the Walkers were—sometimes mated in small herds, but in the opposite manner Kiara's community had. *One female mate for several males!*

Kiara didn't think they could possibly be thinking about her that way. She couldn't imagine they were. After all, she was just some pathetic female they'd found on the side of the road. None of the other males in her community had shown interest in her until Sebastian had, and even then he'd only been interested in coming to her bed one night a week. He hadn't actually been interested in who she was as a person.

She didn't want to be trapped in another 'mate' situation she couldn't get out of.

Although, they didn't frighten her, the way Sebastian sometimes had. In fact, as they filed back in, both she and her doe perked up and she realized she already wanted to see them again. Which *was* frightening, in a way that Sebastian had never scared her.

Maybe it was just some kind of reaction to knowing they'd saved her life. That made sense. After all, no one had ever saved her life before. Of course, they were also just downright attractive, so add in their rescue of her and her surprising attraction was easily explained.

Right?

"Hey beautiful," Gavin said, sliding up to her in the spot right next to her bed Alec had previously taken and made her blink with surprise. He was joking right?

"Um, hello again," she said as they all smiled at her.

A feeling of contentment rose from her doe. She liked having them all there. Kiara just didn't understand why. She prodded her animal and just got a sleepy, unconcerned response.

Like them.

So helpful.

Giving Gavin a dirty look, Alec slid in next to the other man. Kiara noticed he didn't try to challenge Dorian, who took the other closest position to her, on the other side of her bed where he had stood before. Just behind Dorian, Riley smiled encouragingly at her, but remained the quiet one she'd initially labeled him.

"So, now that you're better, where are you headed once you're released?" Gavin asked, his voice casual.

Uh... Kiara actually hadn't thought about that. After all, she hadn't really been sure she'd be cured. She'd been so focused on getting here...

She'd been living in Carson, New Mexico, hiding from Sebastian when he'd found her. At some point when she was fleeing him, heading north into Colorado, she'd contracted the Scourge. It was pure luck she'd made it most of the way to Lakewood before her car broke down, close enough to the facility for her to try to walk. After she'd left her community and talked to other shifters, who obviously hadn't realized she was a small shifter doe, Lakewood had been all the buzz because of the vaccines they'd recently been coming out with, which were supposed to inoculate the smaller shifter populations from the diseases killing them. There had even been whispers of a cure, although the vaccines couldn't fix those who were already sick.

It had been her only hope and she'd taken it, without really considering what came next.

"Ah..." she said, a long awkward moment later when they were still patiently waiting for some kind of answer.

"We're going on vacation," Alec said, apparently without the patience of the others. "If you want to come with us. Ouch." Gavin had elbowed him in the side and was now glaring at him.

"What did we say about playing it cool?" Gavin hissed at him. Maybe if Kiara wasn't a shifter she wouldn't have been able to hear him, but as it was, she could hear him perfectly clearly and it made her want to giggle. They were acting like they liked her. Like something out of one of the books she'd read.

"I'm always cool," Alec said grumpily, rubbing his side where Gavin had elbowed him.

"All evidence to the contrary," Riley chimed in for the first time, teasing his brother. Kiara was fascinated watching the dynamics of their interactions; so silly but so affectionate.

"Ignore them," Dorian advised, reaching out to take her hand. "Except the first thing Alec said. We would like to invite you to come with us while you recover. We're going to a cabin, not too far from here, but it is secluded and there is plenty of space both inside and outside. I know we're strangers, but anyone here will be happy to vouch for us, all you have to do is ask. You'd be perfectly safe with us."

Four faces looked at her, full of eager anticipation.

She didn't understand. On the other hand, did it really matter if she understood? Once the hospital released her, she didn't have anywhere else to go. She was going to have to throw herself at someone's mercy, and they *were* offering.

"Do you have a computer there? And the internet?" she found herself asking.

"Oh yes," Riley said, lighting up. All of them had brightened, grinning encouragingly. Kiara had never been confronted with so much group approval, it was a little daunting. "And Wi-Fi."

So she'd be able to continue her work. Access her bank accounts. Find a new place to live.

"Just for a few days," she said, already feeling guilty for taking advantage of their generosity, even though they'd offered. "Once I'm released."

They all beamed at her with surprise and delight, and she couldn't help but smile back.

******

The cabin was every bit as large as Dorian had claimed, with six bedrooms upstairs, a huge downstairs main room with a massive television, sectional sofa, and kitchen along the other wall. Separated from the main living room, kitchen combination room were two bathrooms, a home office, and a garage full of power tools. In the basement there was a pool table, a wall full of workout equipment, and another television hooked up to video game consoles.

Completely shocked, Kiara had barely spoken throughout the tour.

"I thought you said this was a cabin," she said accusingly, spinning around in the guest bedroom they'd taken her to. "This is a mansion!"

They shrugged, exchanging glances. Something she'd noticed they did quite a lot, as if there was an unspoken conversation happening which she was not privy to.

Rubbing his hand along the back of his head, Gavin gave her a kind of sheepish smile. "I mean, it is large... but you know, with four of us we need plenty of space and we more than make enough to afford it."

"So you'll be okay in here?" Dorian asked and Kiara shook her head in disbelief.

"Okay?" she asked, throwing out her arms in all the space. "My old—" She cut the words off before she could finish the sentence, all too aware of how different her life had been from theirs, even before she'd left her community. From Jesse's reactions and explanations, as well as their reactions to some of the things she'd said, she'd quickly picked up that the way she and the other Pudu deer lived was not considered normal by their standards. Kiara didn't want to be different, she didn't want to stand out, and she certainly didn't want them to know how *not* normal she was.

Even if their opinions shouldn't matter to her, since she was only going to be here a few days, after all. Dr. Tran had released her from the hospital, saying resting and the outdoors would do her a world of good while she recovered and got used to her new hybrid doe. She was apparently going to need to sleep a lot, and Dr. Tran definitely approved having others around to keep an eye on her, just in case any complications cropped up. But Kiara knew she couldn't stay longer than she had to.

Already she could feel them weaving the same spell around her that Sebastian had at the beginning when she'd first been thrilled to be chosen as a mate. Any attention from him at all, and she'd lapped it up, thinking it meant things it didn't. The four stags were already more attentive to her than he had ever been, but they might be that way with all females. Especially since they seemed to feel responsible for her after rescuing her.

Now all four of them were looking at her curiously, probably wondering what she'd been about to say. She smiled tightly. "It's wonderful, thank you."

Riley studied her, like she was some kind of fascinating specimen, as the other three did another one of their little looks. Those looks could get annoying, she decided. Although they were kind of cute too. Ugh. She was tired again and it was making her cranky.

Right on cue, she yawned and reached up to cover her open mouth with her hand.

"We should let you get some rest," Dorian said quickly, looking at the others and nodding to the door. "Let us know if you need anything."

They shuffled out the door, all giving her various versions of the same smile as they went. Dorian's was reassuring and protective, Gavin's playfully charming, Riley's almost wistful and somehow quiet even though he was just smiling, and Alec winked at her along with shooting her a grin. Shaking her head, Kiara collapsed on the bed, thankful she had gotten to shower before leaving the hospital and could just enjoy the huge expanse of the bed.

She felt entirely wrung out, even though she'd already napped once earlier that day. Which was totally normal for her now. Apparently large cat shifters slept a *lot* when they were recovering from any kind of illness or injury, and she was now partially large cat. Add on to that, being completely overwhelmed by her new life, these new men, and all the new thoughts she was having... well, she just needed a break. On this massive, massive bed. She hadn't even known people had beds this large. It could easily fit all four men *and* her.

Eep! With thoughts like that, she must be more tired than she realized.

Closing her eyes, she fell asleep to the sound of deep, rumbling voices a floor below her, soothing both her and her doe and leaving her feeling protected and comforted.

******

When Kiara woke up a couple hours later, the huge 'cabin' was mostly silent. Laying on her back, she listened, but didn't hear anything. Her doe prodded at her, wanting to get up as well, and maybe see if there was some meat in the kitchen downstairs. Kiara made a face at the idea of raw steaks her doe was sending to her, but she got up. Heading to the bathroom, she quickly brushed her teeth and her hair, and pulled the wild mass of hair back into a pony tail. Lakewood had provided her with both toiletries and some clothing before she'd left. They really were quite generous.

Studying her reflection, she pulled her long ponytail over her shoulder to see the full effect of her hair. She'd dyed it to help her hide from Sebastian, but she hadn't been able to bear the thought of cutting it. The very pale blonde didn't look terrible, really, she thought, tilting her head at her reflection. It made her eyes look very large and her skin paler for some reason, but it was not unattractive. Especially since it was now clean.

Food.

Right, yes, food. Prompted by her doe, Kiara left the bathroom and headed down the stairs. Even though her doe was more confident than before, she was still alert to any unusual sounds. Someone was watching the television, and she relaxed as she saw Alec's head swivel to see her from where he was sitting on the couch. Not that she felt unsafe with any of the men—she was definitely at least partially chalking that up to her doe's newfound jaguar confidence—but they did make her feel a bit nervous. Alec was the least intimidating to her, just because of his natural friendliness and exuberance.

"Hey! You're awake. How are you feeling?" he asked, jumping up from where he was sitting and coming over to see her.

He loomed over her, even larger than Sebastian had been, but it didn't scare her at all. Kiara couldn't help but wonder if her doe realized that being a jaguar didn't help Kiara at all when she was in human form. She was just as vulnerable as any other shifter when not shifted.

"Rested, thank you. Um, maybe a little hungry," she said shyly.

Alec's face lit up, surprising her. "Of course, here, come sit down, I'll get you something to eat."

For the next twenty minutes, Kiara was treated to the bewildering and really rather wonderful experience of having a male make her a meal and fuss over her. It was just a sandwich, but she hadn't had anyone make her a meal since she'd been mated. Even before then, her mother had taught her how to cook so she could take care of herself and her mate. She wasn't even sure Sebastian knew how to cook; it certainly wouldn't ever be expected of him. He'd definitely never fussed over her. If she were on her monthlies and cramping or sore, he still expected her to take care of him, never the other way around.

But Alec wouldn't even let her help. He sat her down at the counter, got her a glass of water, and made her a sandwich, chattering to her about the cabin and his brother and cousins the entire time. Apparently Dorian had gone to check out the property, the way he always did when they first arrived, making sure there had been no intruders while they were away and everything looked normal. Gavin was also napping, although he had shifted form and gone outside to his favorite place to do so, and Riley was in the garage tinkering with 'something.' Alec didn't seem very interested in exactly what his brother was doing, but Kiara felt her curiosity rising. If she had a besetting sin, it was surely her desire to always want to 'know.'

Which was how she ended up asking Alec questions she hadn't intended to ask as they ate their sandwiches. He had seated himself beside her after preparing their food and his elbow kept brushing hers as they ate. The light touch was distracting, but in a pleasant way. There were little tingles in her stomach that didn't seem to have anything to do with her hunger, because they kept increasing rather than going away as she ate.

"So... Jesse told me some things about deer herds, like you and your brother and cousins..." she said, her voice trailing off. She blushed as Alec looked up to meet her gaze, his own expression open and friendly. Since Jesse hadn't known for sure, Kiara figured her ignorance might not be too strange even though she was a deer too. Pudu deer and red deer were obviously different. "Um... she said... that you might mate... um..."

"As a herd?" Alec asked, prompting her. Kiara felt her face flush bright red but she couldn't help it. She wanted to know the answer, so she nodded. Alec winked at her cheekily. "Yes, I'm pretty sure we will."

The immediate feeling of jealousy rushing through her was startling, but Kiara pushed it away. Her doe made an odd growling noise in her head.

"How will you know when you've found her?" she asked. The tingles in her stomach had finally disappeared and had been replaced by an odd sinking feeling. Jesse had explained that some shifters found their 'fated mate' and their animals supposedly knew immediately when they'd found each other. Although Jesse hadn't experienced it, one of her mate's siblings had. Other shifters fell in love and claimed each other, usually using a bite... but Jesse hadn't been sure what a deer herd mating would look like. She hadn't known anything about them at all.

"Weeell..." Alec drawled out the word, setting down the quarter of a sandwich he hadn't already devoured. He swiveled on his stool until he was facing her, leaning one elbow against the counter, placing the other on the back of her stool. Kiara felt breathless as he basically caged her in, but not with fear... her pulse was starting to race, and her lungs were tightening, but in a good way somehow. She felt her eyes widening as he leaned in towards her, his voice lowering to a seductive murmur that had her leaning in closer as well, so she could hear him better. "For one, we'd all have to be attracted to her. Our stags would have to be attracted to her as well. We'd want to get to know her. To court her. Show her what life with us could be like. And then when the time came, we'd claim her the way deer shifters do."

Kiara was beginning to feel dizzy she was so breathless. Leaning in closer to Alec, he leaned in towards her as well, and she thought he might kiss her at any moment. Some part of her was screaming out a warning, saying she should pull back now, insisting this was a terrible idea and not to fall for his lines, but the rest of her just wanted this moment. This one moment, even if it never happened again when she felt like the heroine in the books she loved so much, where she felt desirable, and hopeful, like anything could happen, and happily-ever-afters were possible.

"How do deer shifters claim their mates?" She whispered the question, because she couldn't get enough air in her lungs to be any louder, and she didn't need to be anyway with how close Alec was to her.

His gaze dropped to her lips. "Well, it would start with something like this."

Then he leaned in and kissed her.

Softly.

Gently.

A moment later his hand came up to cradle her cheek, making her gasp with surprise and delight at his tender touch, and his tongue slid into her mouth, coaxing a response from hers. He didn't jam it between her lips or make her feel like she was choking on him like Sebastian. He just teased and curled and seduced.

And Kiara felt her whole body begin to tingle, her doe practically whimpering with need inside of her head.

She practically crawled onto his lap, making him groan as his hands wrapped around her waist, holding her tighter. In her head, Kiara's doe was elated, urging her on as she straddled his legs, pressing her scent all over his body.

******

Walking into the house, Gavin was both surprised, delighted, and a little worried to see Alec and Kiara kissing.

Not that Alec seemed to be the aggressor in this situation. Although his hands were on Kiara's cute little butt, it definitely looked like he was just making sure she didn't slide off of his lap as she hungrily kissed him.

The men had all agreed to hang back and make sure Kiara felt safe with them, to take their time with her. She seemed very naive in a lot of ways. While they were all happy she had decided to come with them, it was a little worrying she'd been so willing to trust them and had said yes before even asking Dr. Tran about it. At least she'd asked the doctor eventually, but still. They were thrilled, because they wanted her to trust them and she definitely should, they would never harm her, but also concerned because what if this was just how she was?

And now she was practically riding his cousin's lap with what looked like inexperienced enthusiasm.

Gavin's cock swelled with envy and desire as he watched the pair continue making out, heard the little whimpering noises Kiara was making in the back of her throat.

Ours, his stag said smugly. All of them had admitted their stags were becoming pushier about wanting her.

For deer herds who mated together, the process for mating could be a little different than for other shifters who mated singularly. After all, there were multiple animals, all of whom had to be in agreement. Gavin couldn't help but wonder if their animal sides were communicating with each other somehow, because they had all definitely decided on Kiara and they were all becoming pushier. Fortunately, in this case, none of their human counterparts objected to mating the pretty doe, they just wanted to take things slowly. Alec would have been the most likely one to balk, since he wasn't usually into commitment, but he'd been on board immediately.

They all felt there was something special about her, and with their deer becoming more insistent at the back of their minds all they could do was hope to win her over.

Looked like Alec had a good start at least.

Gavin cleared his throat.

And then started forward, hands outreached even though he was across the room, as Kiara shrieked and nearly tumbled off of Alec's lap. His cousin managed to catch her before she could fall to the floor, but she came way too close to completely face-planting. Face flushed a hot pink, Kiara squirmed away from Alec's hold to stand on her own about a foot away from him. Gavin couldn't help but smirk at the younger man, who seemed a bit at a loss after her reaction.

"Hi. Oh... um, hi Gavin," Kiara said, her words practically tripping over themselves. "I was um... Alec made me lunch and we... um..."

His lips curved up into a smile. She was utterly adorable.

"You were kissing," he said, teasing gently. "I hope you didn't stop on my account. I was enjoying the show, I just wasn't sure you knew you had an audience."

If she had been pink before, now she was scarlet red, the color creeping down her neck and up into her hairline. Her gaze skittered away but she kept peeking at him, checking to see his reaction, as if she thought it might change. Wringing her hands in front of her, it was obvious she was worried about something.

Jumping up, Alec put his arm around her waist, comfortingly. "It's okay sweetheart. I told you about how deer herds mate, remember? We do things together. Especially Gavin, he likes to watch."

"Yes I do," Gavin said easily, enjoying the curious little peeks Kiara was giving him now. She no longer seemed anxious, just... interested. He could work with interested. "Not Alec so much though, his technique leaves a lot to be desired."

"My technique is just fine," Alec said. He tugged Kiara into his side, startling her into looking up at him with wide eyes so he could drop a kiss on her lips. Gavin gave him a stern look when Alec looked at him again.

They were supposed to be taking things *slow*.

Even if she had been crawling on top of Alec, she was obviously still a little skittish.

"I've got some stuff to go take care of," Alec said cheerfully, ignoring Gavin's look and releasing his hold on Kiara's waist. "Gavin will take good care of you though."

******

With Alec gone, Kiara climbed back up onto her chair to finish her sandwich. He'd taken what was left of his with him. She felt incredibly awkward.

Not only had she practically thrown herself at Alec, but his cousin had walked in on them. Neither of the males seemed to feel at all awkward. Neither did her doe. The silly creature was pleased as punch about having made out with Alec, swishing her little tail with smug relish, and hadn't even bothered to alert Kiara to Gavin's presence.

Only Kiara felt awkward.

"What's wrong beautiful?" Gavin asked, picking up Alec's plate and taking it to the sink, cleaning up after his cousin. Kiara watched in wonderment as he rinsed the plate off and put it in the dishwasher.

"I... I didn't mean to kiss Alec," she whispered, embarrassed but also bursting with the need to talk about it, and Gavin was the only person there.

Gavin frowned, his gaze turning dark as he looked towards the door Alec had just exited through. "I thought... I'll have a word with him. He won't bother you again."

"Oh... I..." As Gavin's dark brown eyes turned to focus on her, softening as he took in her anxious expression, Kiara found herself blushing again as she realized he'd misinterpreted. "He wasn't bothering me, I just... um... oh dear."

The look in Gavin's eyes lightened even more, sparkling with amusement. "Oh dear or oh *deer?*" he asked, his emphasis on the word making the pun clear and she couldn't help but giggle, even if it was an awful pun.

"I just meant I hadn't meant to kiss him the way I did," she confessed, still smiling. Both Alec and Gavin were good at making her smile, even when she felt uncomfortable. "I..."

Now she floundered again, because the truth was she'd gotten caught up in the moment. Caught up in feeling like she was desirable, like she mattered. Caught up in being touched. And her doe had definitely not helped either.

Even now, she could feel her doe eyeing Gavin like he was a particularly tasty piece of pie. Grinning, he leaned on the counter across from her, with no idea how close he was to getting jumped on. Kiara didn't know if her hormones were out of control, or if this was a side effect of her doe becoming a hybrid (and also a floozy apparently), or if she was just that desperate for any male attention and affection. She was very worried it might be the last option motivating her the most.

"I don't want another mate," she blurted out.

Gavin blinked. A frown lines began to form on his forehead. "*Another* mate?"

The flush that washed over her now wasn't embarrassment, it felt more like shame. Kiara averted her eyes from him, nodding.

"Sweetie..." Gavin came around the side of the counter so he was next to her, his fingers sliding under her chin and tilting her head back to look at him. "You aren't mated."

"Yes I am," she said, scowling at him.

To her supreme annoyance, his lips twitched in amusement. "No, you aren't. Your doe wouldn't have let you kiss Alec if that had been the case, and we would smell a male's scent mixed with yours."

"Jesse said deer are a little different," she argued crossly. She did *not* appreciate being told she didn't have a mate. Of course she did, otherwise what had she been doing with Sebastian all this time?

Tilting his head, Gavin opened his mouth and started to say something, then closed it. He looked at her, obviously thinking hard. "Sweetheart, why don't you tell me why you think you're mated."

Her temper stoked just enough to not care that the way her community found mates was apparently different from everyone else, she told him about Sebastian.

Chapter 4

Almost as soon as Riley came in the door, Gavin sprinted out, practically bursting out of his skin and into his stag. He nearly stumbled, he shifted so quickly, but managed to get himself balanced before hitting the woods, bounding away in a flash of red fur and antlers.

Concerned, Riley turned back into the house. "Kiara?"

"I'm here." The glum response made his step quicken. She was sitting at the counter, poking what looked like the crust of a sandwich. As he came closer she looked up, her expression sad. Riley wasn't sure what had Gavin in such a state, but obviously it had something to do with Kiara. He'd gotten the text message from Gavin, asking Riley to come and cover his shift with the doe, and immediately hurried over. It wasn't like Gavin to call for someone to relieve him of a duty.

"Is everything okay?" he asked, feeling awkward and uncertain as he moved toward her. She looked so sad, but Riley didn't know what to do. Should he hug her? Pat her back? Keep his distance? It all depended on what was making her sad, so he needed more information.

"I think I made Gavin angry," she said morosely, still poking her sandwich crust instead of looking at him. Riley moved over to sit on the stool next to her. He didn't argue with her assessment. The evidence certainly indicated Gavin was upset at the very least and, as Riley had not been present for the inciting incident, Kiara's hypothesis had more weight than any guess he could make. His stag roused, pressing against his mind and insisting he fix whatever the problem was.

"How did you do that?" he asked. Hopefully if he knew what had happened he could work through to a solution. Also, he had a fair amount of curiosity running rampant, since it took quite a bit to work Gavin up into a lather.

As Kiara sadly told him about her 'mate' and her old community, Riley understood why Gavin had called him for backup instead of Dorian or Alec. While her story had probably sent Gavin into a roaring fury, it would have deranged Dorian, and Alec was a complete hothead. They'd both have been shouting and ranting before she'd even finished, and that was obviously not what their pretty doe needed right now. Riley would not consider himself the first choice for comforting anyone—he knew he didn't always relate very well to people outside of his brother and cousins—but he was at least able to hold on to his rising fury.

"Is it true?" she asked him tearfully, straining his resolve to remain calm and logical for her, looking up at him with big, Bambi eyes. "I wasn't actually mated to him? It was just... just breeding? The whole community, everything they said was a lie?"

"Yes," he said, as gently as he could, now wishing he had some back up as her lower lip quivered. Her lashes fluttered as she blinked faster, trying to hold back tears. Riley spoke quickly, hoping to get all the information out and stem the threatening distress. "Although different shifter types do sometimes differ in their mating, there is always a marker to indicate when a mating has occurred, to warn off other possibly interested parties—oh please don't do that..."

Feeling utterly helpless, he held out his hands to her as she burst into tears.

"Sorry... sorry..." she said, sniffling and gulping and obviously trying to hold back her overflowing emotions and stifle her sobs.

She's leaking! His stag jabbed at him, both startled and upset. *Fix her!*

Riley was distressed enough he couldn't even be amused at his animal's description of her tears.

What would Dorian do? Riley asked himself helplessly, wishing he had one of his take-charge cousins here to help, or even his younger brother. Alec was good at cheering people up. He definitely hadn't meant to make her think she couldn't cry. Riley could start there.

"No, I'm sorry," he said, standing up and pulling her into a hug. Hugs were good. Crying females liked hugs. She nuzzled against him and his deer chuffed in approval. Okay, so far so good. "You can cry. I shouldn't have asked you not to." He patted the back of her head awkwardly and the smell of strawberries rose up from her hair. It was nice. Actually, just having her snuggled up to him was nice. Except for the crying. That part wasn't nice at all.

They had all agreed to take their time with her, but she seemed to need the physical comfort. Her arms had wrapped around him and she was burrowing into his chest like it was a den and she was ready to hibernate.

Making a snap decision—not his usual forte, but with the anxious pushing of his stag it seemed a logical route—Riley guided her away from the kitchen counter and over to the couch where he could at least hold her more comfortably. To his relief, she didn't seem at all upset by the relocation and the rate of her weeping reduced much faster as he cradled her on his lap. Physical contact seemed to be key, something which he made a mental note of for the future.

As she calmed, so did his stag, much to his relief. Of course, while he had calmed emotionally, his physical reaction was quite different. He was far too aware of her rounded bottom nestled into his lap, her breasts pressed against his chest, and the scent of strawberries from her shampoo wafting around him. Riley prayed she didn't notice the hardening shaft pressing against her thigh. He liked having her cuddled up to him like this and he didn't want to give her a reason to move.

"You're very nice," she murmured, snuggling in, her head pressed against his shoulder. Riley's protective urges soared, reflecting on everything she'd been through. Not just since becoming stricken with the Scourge, but before that. Her upbringing sounded very unusual and not at all conducive to being independent or free-thinking, and yet she had escaped even knowing she'd be risking her life by doing so, determined to make a new start. He didn't think he'd ever met someone so strong or brave before. There was no way to actually quantify such traits, of course, but he knew it was true.

Her even breathing indicated she'd fallen asleep again. Dr. Tran had warned them she would be quite tired, eating and sleeping a lot as her body recovered. Terrified to wake her, Riley froze in place.

He'd seen memes online about people refusing to move after their pet crawled onto their lap, but he'd never understood why until now.

Not that Kiara was a pet.

Riley made a mental note never to speak the comparison aloud.

******

The sound of the door opening and male voices woke Kiara. She was so warm and comfortable it took her a moment to remember everything that had happened before she fell asleep. And another moment to realize she was *still* on Riley's lap, in his arms. Squeaking, she vaulted up.

Or, well, she tried to.

His leanly muscled arms were still wrapped around her body, meaning she only got about halfway through her leap before she was yanked back down as he came awake with a jerk of startled surprise.

"Sorry, didn't mean to startle you," Alec said, breezing over to drop a kiss on the top of her head, completely fine that she was sitting on his brother's lap, in his arms, even though she'd been kissing *him* earlier. "Were you taking a nap?"

"Yes, I was tired," she said, a bit shyly as Gavin followed Alec over.

"Hey beautiful," he said, also dropping a kiss on her head, also completely fine with her position on Riley's lap. "I'm sorry I ran out earlier. I was just so angry at all the people who treated you terribly and my stag was so riled, I had to get out and run."

"You weren't angry with me?" she asked, both surprised and delighted, before remembering she had decided she wasn't going to get attached to these men. Any of them. She was still on the run from Sebastian—with no way of knowing whether or not he was still chasing her—and she didn't really know them. No matter how she was drawn to them or attracted to them, it was a bad idea. There were four of them after all; she hadn't been able to ever keep Sebastian's attention for a full night. Even if they thought they were interested in her now, she'd never be able to satisfy one of these virile, confident, sexy men, much less all of them. It was better to protect herself and keep away.

Wasn't it?

Gavin lifted her up from Riley's lap and over the back of the couch, making her squeak at the sudden movement. She opened her mouth to protest, only to find her lips suddenly occupied with a smoldering hot kiss that had all of her anxieties and self-doubts fleeing in the face of sudden, passionate desire.

She felt a little dizzy when he released her, her body even warmer than it had been when she first woke up. Setting her on her feet, Gavin gave her a wink.

"Not even a little bit angry at *you,* sweetie."

Relief suffused her, and then a spark of disappointment as Dorian headed into the kitchen, sending her nothing more than a smile. Her doe huffed in disapproval.

Darn it. She shouldn't be disappointed about that!

Pushing aside her wanton desires, Kiara went to offer her help.

Dinnertime was a revelation. Not only did all of the males contribute to the making of the meal—not allowing her to do more than sit at the counter and chop vegetables for them (she wasn't going to tire herself out *that* quickly, but they insisted)—but they took their time over dinner to entertain her. Funny stories about growing up together, a lot of stories about Gavin and Alec's prank wars, descriptions of their own families (Gavin and Dorian "only" had two fathers, Alec and Riley had five!), and very gentle questions about her own life. If she hesitated too much or became reticent, they quickly picked up the thread of conversation until she was giggling helplessly again.

Gavin and Alec were definitely the two entertainers, while Riley was the quietest, and Dorian fulfilled what she thought of as the 'fatherly' role. Which made her think of one of the very *naughty* books she'd edited for work—Daddy Dorian would make a great book. She'd read it. So often she'd escaped into one of the books she'd been sent to edit, where people's lives were so much more enjoyable than the life she'd been living. Her dinners had mostly been eaten alone. Even when she had eaten with the others in her community, it hadn't been like this. The other Pudu deer females had all eaten mostly quietly, content in their solitude and not wanting real connections with each other. Maybe because they had all been competing for attention from the same males.

She was practically crying from laughing so hard when Alec aimed a spoonful of peas at Gavin, threatening him from across the table, while Dorian frowned sternly and warned him he better not in a deeply imposing voice which seemed to give Alec second thoughts but not entirely intimidate him. A moment later the peas dropped all over Alec's lap because Riley had jostled his elbow, grinning wickedly. Quiet but sneaky, that was Riley, Kiara decided.

Sweet too. She still couldn't quite believe he'd just sat there for two hours, eventually falling asleep himself, just so he wouldn't disturb her while she napped. When she'd asked him about it earlier, he'd just kind of shrugged sheepishly and mumbled something about her being too cute to move, before quickly hurrying away to work on his contribution to dinner.

At the end of the meal she helped clear the table, but was quickly sent to sit down again because it was "Alec's turn" to do dishes. Kiara thought it made sense for them all to take turns when they had just been a bachelor herd, but she was still a little confused when they didn't let her just take over the chore now. Shouldn't they want her to?

She also didn't feel like she was pulling her weight.

"You're our guest, you are not going to do chores," Dorian said, so firmly that she had to bite her lip against replying 'yes, daddy.' Her body was all kinds of riled up and her doe wasn't helping, but she hadn't completely lost her mind. Yet.

The other three taught her how to play poker while Alec did the dishes before joining them. Kiara had heard of the game before, but had never played it, and she enjoyed it even though she was terrible at it. Just like over dinner, the men were silly and fun, mocking each other, affectionately competing, and calling each other names. They didn't call her any names, but they still teased her about her easy-to-read expressions when she had a really good or bad hand.

When she tried to pout, to pretend she had a bad hand instead of a 'full house' as they'd called it, Gavin burst out laughing.

"That is the fakest pout I've ever seen," he said, reaching out to poke at her lower lip. Squealing, Kiara smacked his hand away instinctively—and then froze, deer-in-the-headlights. But he didn't yell or get angry, he was still laughing as he leaned back, and the icy sensation of terror quickly trickled away. The others were chuckling too, Riley staring at his cards, Alec looking at Gavin... Kiara focused on her cards and tried to ignore Dorian's intent stare as he studied her, seeing far more than she wanted him to.

******

A knock had Kiara looking up to see Gavin standing in her doorway, rapping his knuckles against the frame. She was sitting up in her bed, a laptop in front of her so she could check her emails and try to catch up on her work before going to sleep. Thankfully she hadn't missed any deadlines while she was ill, but she was going to have to work her tail off to make the upcoming ones, and she definitely couldn't afford to lose any money now.

"Hey," he said, giving her what was probably his most charming grin. Kiara melted a little bit under the force of it and she could hear her doe practically purring in her head. Her doe had definitely never purred before. Was that an effect of the jaguar genes or just her doe's obvious interest in the four Walker stags? "Can I come in?"

After a moment of shocked surprise that he was asking, Kiara belatedly nodded her head. "Yes, of course."

He sauntered in and sat down on her bed, only a few feet away from her, with his legs off of the side but his upper body turned towards her. Reaching out with his hand, he leaned back into a comfortable position. Kiara felt a hot flush between her legs as her tummy started to flutter.

Whenever any of the men were around her, it was so hard to remember all the reasons she had for not becoming attached to them.

"I just wanted to apologize again for running out the way I did this afternoon," he said seriously, his dark brown eyes almost soulful. "I definitely didn't mean to make you think I was upset with you. You're amazing. I was upset on your behalf, but when it comes to you, I'm just in awe. You're so brave and you've been through so much, and yet you're still incredibly sweet and kind."

These men sure knew how to make her blush. She didn't think she'd been so pink since the first romance book she'd read for her job. Kiara didn't really know how to respond. She certainly didn't feel brave. Desperation had driven her when she'd run away. Could running away really be called brave?

"You don't have to apologize," she said, running her hands over the sheets covering her lap. "I'm just a guest here, you all have been wonderful about keeping me entertained, but if you needed a minute to yourself... I mean... it's fine, of course. No apology necessary." Good, now she was repeating herself as she babbled. Her blush ran hotter, this time from embarrassment as Gavin grinned at her.

"Well I did anyway, now say 'apology accepted, Gavin.'"

"Apology accepted, Gavin," she parroted obediently, a smile lifting her lips in amusement.

"Good. Now, I think we should kiss and make up," he said, scooting closer as Kiara's heart began to pound. Wide eyed, she stared at him, breathless... waiting. Some part of her felt cynical, sure he was going to push to have sex with her now, but he just lowered his lips to hers and kissed her.

Gently.

Sweetly.

Like he was cherishing the feel of his lips against hers. Like all he wanted to do was kiss her. Just like with Alec earlier. Kiara moaned, leaning into the kiss, wanting more, just like she had with Alec. Her doe purred with approval, urging Kiara onward.

When Gavin started to pull back, Kiara clung to him, only then realizing that her hands had moved up to his chest, her fingers holding on to his shirt. His dark eyes were hot, lustful... but he was gently reaching up to pluck her hands away.

"Kiara..." He rasped her name, his voice husky as his fingers slid between hers. He'd removed her hands from his chest but didn't seem quite able to let her go. Kiara knew how he felt. "I didn't come in here for... I don't want you to think I'm just interested in you for..." His voice kept trailing off.

She thought she understood what he was trying to say, even if she didn't understand *why* he would feel that way. It was so far and away from what she would expect, from what she was used to, she couldn't quite comprehend his reasoning. But she also knew she didn't want him to go.

Her body ached in a way it never had for Sebastian, her doe interested in and encouraging the proceedings in a manner she'd never exhibited before. Despite all the very good reasons she had for not wanting to get attached, Kiara really wanted to forget all those arguments she'd come up with. Just for right now. Gavin seemed willing to do whatever *she* wanted. When could she be sure she would ever get this chance again?

Maybe he would have pity on her if she just asked. He thought she was brave, so she would be brave and say what she really, truly, secretly wanted.

"Will you stay with me tonight?" She could hear the plea in her voice. "Please? All night?"

Just once, she wanted to sleep with a man in bed with her. Maybe even snuggling with her, the way she'd read about humans doing. Her heart sank, her shoulders hunching in when he didn't answer immediately and she tried to pull her hands away, but he wouldn't let her go.

"It's not that I don't want to," he said gently, keeping his fingers laced through hers, using them to pull her towards him instead of letting her curl into a little ball of embarrassment. "I'm just not sure why you're asking."

"I don't want to be alone." The truth blurted from her lips before she could stop to think how pathetic she sounded. Because she wasn't just talking about not wanting to be alone tonight. She was talking her whole life up until this moment. While her mother had been loving, she also hadn't been a physically affectionate person, which was something Kiara found herself craving more and more as she'd grown up.

The four Walkers had already given her touch-starved senses more satisfaction than her mother and Sebastian combined. The way Alec had held her, Riley had held her, and now Gavin—refusing to let go of her hands. Only Dorian had been standoffish about touching her, but she was used to that.

What she wanted was more of what Gavin was already giving her, more of being held while she slept, like Riley had done. But... without the panic when she'd been startled awake.

"Okay, sweetheart," Gavin said, his eyes softening. "I'll stay. Just, give me a minute to go change and I'll be right back."

Keeping her squeal of delighted excitement quiet, Kiara let his hands go when he pulled them away and watched him exit the room, her heart pounding as she put the laptop on the nightstand. Part of her was sure he was gone and wouldn't be back, but she was finding it easier and easier not to listen to that part of herself. The self-doubting, insecure part who thought she shouldn't put her heart out on the line again, not after what had happened with Sebastian.

These males were nothing like Sebastian. They liked her. They *showed* her they liked her. And she felt safe with them. Cherished. Even though she hadn't realized Sebastian had lied about actually mating her, that the female deer in her community hadn't had real mates, she'd definitely never felt this way with him. And she'd been one of his so-called 'mates' for almost two years before she'd left.

Still, even with her doe and her logical side pushing down her doubt, she still felt a wave of relief when Gavin came back in to her room and shut the door behind him. It was immediately followed by a wave of desire. He'd changed into a pair of grey sweatpants and a white tank top which clung to his upper body and did very little to hide the bulk of his muscles. This was the most Kiara had ever seen of a man who wasn't Sebastian.

Sebastian had similar musculature to Gavin, but he definitely hadn't sent her doe into a frenzy the way the animal was now. Kiara surreptitiously wiped her hand over her mouth just to make sure she wasn't drooling. Her thighs were pressed tightly together underneath the covers as her lower body pulsed with need.

We're not fulfilling that need tonight, she reminded herself and her doe, ignoring the little huffy sound her animal made. She'd asked Gavin to just sleep with her and he'd made it pretty clear he wasn't here for sex.

Sitting in the middle of the huge bed, which somehow already felt smaller even though he wasn't in it with her yet, Kiara felt remarkably shy. She didn't really know what to do or say.

Gavin just sauntered over to the bed and lifted up the covers to climb in. Part of her felt like she should scoot over, but there was really plenty of space even with her in the middle. Scooting over would be silly.

So instead of moving over, she moved down so she was lying flat on her back, feeling stiff and awkward. Gavin chuckled, turning out the light on the bedside table as he slid between the sheets.

It felt like all the air had squeezed out of her lungs when she felt his large, hot body moving beside hers.

"Relax, beautiful," he said, finding the top of her head even in the darkness as he curled his body around hers. Kiara nearly whimpered at the feel of hard muscles tensing and moving against her body, and then let out a little squeak as she was turned onto her side and pulled so her back was pressed up against his front.

The rigid length of his erection pressed against her buttocks, and she waited for him to do something... but he just lay there. Holding her.

Hand on her stomach.

Nose in her hair.

His breathing slow and regular.

It felt amazing.

Breathing with him, she could feel both herself and her doe relaxing. The need to sleep rose up, overcoming her physical arousal, and she dropped off to sleep in his arms.

******

Mmmmm. Kiara's body was hot with desire and she undulated against a hard male body.

Sebastian? In bed with her while she was asleep?

"Kiara... wake up, beautiful." A soft groan. "Kiara, I need you to wake up sweetheart, you're killing me."

The husky voice was definitely not Sebastian's. Sebastian would have never stayed the night in her bed anyway.

Gavin.

His body against hers, hips rocking against her soft belly, hard cock throbbing between their bodies. Kiara's eyes flew open, but all she could see was tank top, man chest, and a little bit of dark chest hair.

She and Gavin were pressed front to front and she was clinging to him, with both arms and legs. Kiara almost pulled away, embarrassed, but... he felt so good.

Her body undulated again, rolling her mound against the length of his cock and making him groan again, his hands tightening on her back.

"Kiara... sweetheart, that's not nice," he said, his voice strained with pent-up desire.

"Maybe I don't want to be nice," she murmured, squirming against him to try and get a better position. To try to feel more of him. She rubbed her nose in his chest hair and felt his whole body shudder. "Maybe I want to be a bad girl."

She was just mimicking words she'd read in books, pretty sure she understood the sentiment behind them. It seemed to work.

"Sweet Mother of all that is holy," Gavin muttered under his breath as he rolled both of them over.

Darkly handsome, looming over her, his body between her thighs, rigid cock pressed against her swollen pussy through their clothing, he absolutely took Kiara's breath away. His dark eyes were burning with heat and lust. Now this look she recognized, it was similar to one Sebastian would sometimes give her, but Gavin's expression was so much hotter, so much more intense.

He didn't just look like he wanted to mount her, he looked like he wanted to claim her, to possess her. The tension in his body created an equal tension in her, and she stared up at him—but the sound of knuckles rapping on her bedroom door made her squeak with surprise as Gavin's expression changed to one of chagrined disappointment.

"Don't come in!" she called out, sitting up and clutching the sheets to her chest. Inside her head, her doe was kicking up a serious fuss about being denied the sweet fulfillment she'd been sure was about to come her way.

"Kiara? Is Gavin in there with you?" Dorian's deep voice didn't sound judgmental, but she still winced, blushing and feeling guilty.

"Yeah, I'm here," Gavin said, sighing as he stood up out of the bed. The door opened as Gavin moved towards it, to reveal Dorian standing there. The twins looked at each other, Dorian's goatee twitching slightly at the corner of his mouth. Turning back to Kiara in the bed, Gavin gave her a little smile. "See you later, beautiful."

Blinking, Kiara felt like whining as she watched him walk away. They'd just slept together all night, she'd had his hard cock pressed up against her body, and... that was it? Her doe snarled in agitated disbelief.

"Good morning, beautiful," Dorian said, echoing his twin's words, although he didn't move from his spot at the door. His dark eyes drank her in the same way though; almost possessive, even from a distance, which Kiara didn't understand at all.

She scowled at him, annoyed both at being interrupted and at his careless assurance. Even if it did look good on him, that didn't make it less frustrating. As much as she wanted to ask him what he wanted, in a way that made it clear his presence was unwelcome, she couldn't quite bring herself to be so rude. No matter how welcome the males all tried to make her feel, this wasn't *her* house, it was theirs'.

"Good morning," she said, although her tone didn't quite match her words. To her supreme annoyance, his teeth flashed as he smiled widely. And he just kept standing there, looking at her. "Was there something you needed from me?"

"No. Just enjoying the view." His gaze drifted down to her breasts, and Kiara yanked the blankets up as soon as she realized her t-shirt did nothing to disguise her hard nipples poking through the fabric. The man's arrogance was breathtaking. Unfortunately, some part of her also found it charming. When his eyes met hers again, his gaze widened, and she frowned in further confusion.

"I thought..." Her voice trailed off. Dorian cocked his head at her, almost daring her to continue. Well, fine then. Her chin tilted up. "I thought you didn't like me."

To Kiara's shock, he didn't respond verbally, instead he strode across the room in a few quick steps and then was leaning over the bed. His hand reached out to catch her braided hair, from which quite a few strands had escaped, and he used it like a piece of rope to reel her in towards him. When their lips were almost touching, her wide eyes staring directly into his, even her doe was struck silent by the sheer, dominant force of his gaze.

"I like you just fine, sweetheart," he said silkily. "But you aren't ready for me yet." Just as abruptly as he'd come in, he released her braid and was off the bed and headed for the door, tossing one last comment over his shoulder. "Get dressed and come on downstairs. I'm making waffles."

Dumbfounded, more than a little turned on, and completely sexually frustrated, Kiara slumped back into the bed. Just for a moment. She was practically dizzy with confusion.

These   males   made   no   sense.

Chapter 5

After taking a shower, during which she found a little bit of relief using her fingers, although it wasn't nearly the release her body was truly craving, Kiara headed downstairs to find Dorian making waffles as promised. Not just regular waffles either, he'd arranged a number of toppings on the counter to top them with. Blueberries, chopped strawberries, miniature chocolate chips, whipped cream, sour cream, caramel sauce, bacon...

She eyed him a little warily, not sure what to think of him. Out of all the men, he was the hardest to read. Especially because she truly thought he was the most standoffish and indifferent to her, but he'd just proved that theory wrong upstairs. Her lips still tingled from the kiss he hadn't delivered.

"Here," he said, holding out a plate with two large waffles already on it. Kiara took it, although she was a little doubtful she'd be able to finish such a huge portion. On the other hand, she was really hungry, and Dr. Tran had told her to try to eat and sleep as much as possible these first few days. So far, she was doing better with the sleeping than with the eating. She piled her waffles high with blueberries, strawberries, and whipped cream but put the slices of bacon on the side.

Yum. Bacon.

"Where is everyone else?" Kiara asked as she sat down at the table. Dorian was only a few steps behind her, seating himself across from her. He'd separated his two waffles out into savory and sweet. One had bacon, sour cream, and chives, the other had strawberries, chocolate chips, and whipped cream. To her amusement, he pushed the 'dessert' waffle to the side and started in on the other one, as if one really was his meal and the other dessert.

"Riley's out tinkering in the garage," Dorian said, jerking his head in the direction of the door leading there. "Gavin's out running a patrol and Alec is still asleep. He had the latest shift."

"The latest shift?" she echoed, a little confused.

"Patrol shift," Dorian explained. The smile he sent her way was reassuring. "We're not too worried about someone from The Company actually knowing where we are, but just in case, one of us will be checking regularly to make sure no one is wandering around on our land."

The possessive, protective way he said 'our land' almost made her feel like he was more interested in keeping any trespassers away than anyone else. Kiara had actually almost forgotten about The Company. Any of the smaller shifters who had been 'cured' by Dr. Montgomery were desperately wanted by the shadowy entity. Secrecy was the easiest way to keep her safe, so as few people as possible knew Kiara was anything but a regular deer. Apparently, the stags felt it was better to be safe than sorry.

So now there were two things to be worried about—Sebastian finding her and The Company finding her. But at least while she was here, she could feel secure.

"Are you all taking turns guarding me too?" she asked, half-teasing and half-curious, because they'd also seemed to have some kind of rotation going on with her.

Dorian grinned at her and winked. "No, we're all taking turns letting you get to know us."

******

Seeing Kiara's pretty mouth drop open in surprise, Dorian couldn't help but think about exactly what he'd like to do to her mouth.

But not yet. She was still recovering, still getting to know all of them, and her life experiences before now had been both harrowing and had left her very innocent in a lot of ways. He wasn't sure she even realized her scent had started to mingle with theirs. All of the men had been comparing notes as they could, keeping each other apprised of each little tidbit they learned about her. It had added up to a fairly alarming picture.

With as skittish as she was, Dorian hadn't been sure how she'd feel about him. He'd done his own little test this morning, and he was pretty sure her response had been submissive excitement, but that didn't mean *she* knew what her reaction had meant. Especially considering her previous experience with the male who had misrepresented himself as her mate, playing on her ignorance. It was enough to make Dorian wish he could go storming off and go rescue all the females she'd left behind.

On the other hand, the Pudu deer's extreme isolationist tactics had also kept their community safe and disease-free, unlike so many of the small shifter communities whose limited contact with others had still led to devastating results. Maybe some of them were just doing the best they could under the circumstances. At least, that was how he felt in his more charitable moments.

In his less charitable moments, he wanted to question Kiara about her 'mate' and go find the man and rend him limb from limb. Let his stag have free rein and make use of his antlers, the way the seething creature wanted to. His buck was very upset at the idea that someone else had dared call Kiara 'mate.'

Gavin would help him bury the body.

Actually, Riley might be the better choice. Not for burying a body, but actually disposing of it in a manner which would destroy all evidence and make identification next to impossible. Riley knew some scary things. Most people assumed that his quiet, scientific nature meant he was less of a threat than the rest of the Walkers; most people assumed very wrongly.

"So, what are we going to do today?" Kiara asked, a little warily, interrupting Dorian's blood-thirsty thoughts.

"Do you need to work?" he asked. She'd mentioned she did all of her work online and he knew she had been worried about falling behind. When she nodded, looking a little relieved, he felt a surge of satisfaction at anticipating her needs. "Alright then, once you're ready to take a break, let me know and we can go for a run. I'm sure your doe would enjoy the woods here."

The way she brightened made him grin. He was looking forward to seeing her doe. All the men had looked up Pudu deer online the moment they'd been able to. Pudu deer looked tiny in the photos, he and his stag were unbearably curious about what she would look like. Especially with the changes made after creating a hybrid. Would any of the jaguar show through?

Although, his curiosity was nothing compared to Riley's. His cousin had already made the request to be informed if they went for a run. Dorian had a feeling Alec would even roll himself out of bed for the opportunity, and he'd be surprised if Gavin *didn't* meet up with them while they were out there.

"We could go for a run now and I could work later," she said almost hopefully.

"Work first, then play, little doe," he said sternly, hiding his amusement as she made a face at him. Rising, empty plate in hand, he went to do his dishes, just barely catching the tongue she stuck out at him.

Sassy little thing. Life hadn't beaten her down at all, no matter what she'd been through. His stag approved. So did Dorian. She was amazing.

While Kiara worked, Dorian pulled up his own emails to make sure everything was going well back at Lakewood, as well as sending Dr. Tran a report on how Kiara's recovery was going. His team leader, Ginny Wright, had sent him an update from Eli. So far, no sign of The Company, no indication that anyone who shouldn't know about Kiara's transformation had any inkling there was another hybrid now running around, and no sign of the rest of Kiara's community. She hinted that Eli was going to want to talk to Kiara eventually, especially about her community. Probably when he wasn't so focused on taking down The Company.

Word was spreading about The Company, as a warning to the shifter population, and so far, almost everyone seemed infuriated by its tactics and wanted the threat gone. He'd heard The Company had somehow managed to recruit some shifters, but anyone with morals wanted nothing to do with a company willing to kidnap, kill, and experiment on people. Eli had become particularly rabid about discovering everything he could and dismantling it after an attack on Cryus Peak a month ago.

There had been a traitor in the Lakewood ranks, leading to the attack on the location where an entire shifter pack had been in hiding, guarding the Bunson sisters as well as two more small shifters successfully turned hybrid. Several good soldiers had been killed in the attack and Eli had come back practically frothing at the mouth.

Dorian was just glad he didn't have to deal with him. He was perfectly happy leading his own small herd while Ginny led the team and dealt with Eli.

It made him feel particularly protective over Kiara. As far as he was concerned, far too many people knew about her existence and her treatment. Unfortunately, Dr. Tran hadn't been the only person in the room when Kiara had explained her small shifter status. He didn't think there were any more traitors at Lakewood, but he was still on edge.

After about two hours of sitting at her computer, Kiara slammed it shut. "I want to go for a run now."

The bossy, demanding way she made her declaration was almost defiant, as if she expected him to tell her 'no.' Instead, he closed his own laptop and got up, reaching out his hand to help her up as well. "Okay, let's go."

Fifteen minutes later, he, Alec, and Riley had shifted into their stags on the front lawn and were waiting for Kiara to come out from around the side of the house. Apparently, she had only ever shifted with females and she'd turned a bright, tomato red when they'd gotten outside and immediately begun stripping.

Squeaking in adorable alarm, she'd scurried around to the side of the house, yelling over her shoulder that she'd shift there and come back. Exchanging glances which were both concerned and amused, none of them voiced any opinions, since she'd probably be able to hear anything they said even if they whispered. Shifters weren't normally body shy, since shifting in clothing wasn't exactly comfortable, so they found her modesty endearing and cute, but it was also a sign of how different her upbringing had been.

Now the three stags were standing and waiting. They could smell her doe as well as her nervousness, and they didn't want to do anything to scare her off, so they just waited patiently.

When she finally came around the side of the building, Dorian was almost overwhelmed by the protective instinct which welled up inside of him.

She was *tiny* compared to their stags. Delicate ears, big eyes, with a muscled but very small body. Only about two feet tall, she could easily stand underneath any of their stags and have room to spare. He went nearly cross eyed at how adorable she was, and even his buck was close to kneeling down just to get on her level and see what it was like. No wonder Pudu deer relied on their ability to hide as their main defense against predators.

As if sensing their patronizing thoughts, Kiara lifted her lip, giving a little snarl that was definitely all jaguar as she showed off her sharp, predator teeth.

His stag stilled, wary but still interested. Little, but obviously not as defenseless as a regular Pudu doe. Not anymore.

Giving a little sniff, Kiara bounded away into the woods, her tiny legs moving wickedly fast and propelling her forward with more force than he would have thought possible.

Holy shit she's fast!

Dorian raced after her, his cousins following just a few steps behind.

******

Run! Run! Freeeeeeee!!!!!

Kiara's doe was practically squealing with glee as she bolted through the forest, while Kiara was in the back of her head wishing she could put on the brakes.

Her doe moved a *lot* faster than she'd been able to previously. It was hard to put her trust in her animal's natural grace and just let her go when it felt like they were whizzing through the forest at break-neck speed.

The glee didn't just come from the fact that she hadn't shifted in a while, but because shifting had always been very controlled back in the commune. Everyone had to stay together for safety, no one could run off on their own... her doe had chafed a little at the restrictions at the time, but Kiara was still pretty sure that part of her excitement now came from the jaguar. She could feel the newness of the predator in her, the thrill of the run, the desire to pounce and chase and hunt.

Behind her, the stags were crashing through the forest much more noisily than she was. They were quite majestic creatures when standing still, her doe had been very struck by the sight of them, but when running through the forest they didn't have half of her elegant dexterity.

A sound ahead of her had her skidding to a halt, her doe wary but also confident. Instead of hiding, the way she would have before her genetics had been altered, she stood her ground, ready and waiting for the threat. Behind her, she could hear the stags catching up. There was a rustle of branches and then suddenly a huge shadow covered her, two muscled deer legs planting down on either side of her head.

Kiara looked up.

Dorian was literally standing over her like a protective behemoth.

If her doe could have rolled her eyes... On the other hand, it was also kind of cute. There was a part of her which got a little melty about his stance, as well as the way Riley and Alec were flanking him. When she'd gone out with the Pudu deer, the females were expected to defend and sacrifice themselves for the males. There were so many fewer males after all.

Fortunately, it had never happened, but Kiara and the others had all known what they were supposed to do. Being the protected one felt both odd and nice. Basically, very similar to how she'd been feeling ever since meeting the Walker stags.

The wind was blowing away from them, so they couldn't scent whoever was approaching them, but as soon as another deer shifter came into view, Kiara relaxed along with the other males. She immediately knew it was Gavin. His stag looked exactly like Dorian's—except Dorian's was maybe a little shaggier around the mouth. Kiara giggled internally, wondering if that was because of Dorian's facial hair.

Now with all of the stags around her, Kiara's doe was happy to explore the woods at a more sedate pace. They ranged around her, one of them always directly next to her (although they took turns) and the others alertly moving ahead of and behind her, keeping an eye out for any possible threats.

Before Kiara felt emotionally ready, she was already getting physically tired. Noticing her slowing pace, Dorian had them turning back for the house. By the time they got there, she couldn't even shift, and Dorian carried her doe upstairs to curl up on her bed still shifted.

******

When Kiara woke up, Alec was on the bed beside her, reading something on his tablet. Curious about what he was reading, and without really thinking about what she was doing, Kiara shifted.

Alec's mouth dropped open and she turned bright pink all over. Which he could see, because she was naked.

"EEK!" Oh god, she'd actually just said 'eek'—could she get more cliché? "I'm sorry! I'm sorry!"

She rolled away from him, trying to cover herself with her hands, but she'd forgotten how big the bed was. Rolling over didn't result in her falling off the bed, the way she'd expected. But at least she was face down with only her butt exposed.

Inside her head, Kiara was pretty sure her doe was laughing at her. Stupid animal. *This isn't funny!*

Her doe just didn't have the same societal conventions about nudity. She didn't understand Kiara's embarrassment.

Yes. Present. Strangely, she felt like wagging her bottom, even though she didn't have a tail attached. That was new. It must be a cat thing. *Let him mount.*

Oh for the love of... *I am not trying to get him to mount me!*

"Uh... Kiara? Are you okay?" Alec asked, his voice sounding hoarse.

Completely crimson, she turned her head just enough to peek at him through the blonde curtain of her hair. He was staring at her butt.

See? Stag wants to mount.

Now her doe was starting to sound petulant. Kiara knew how she felt.

But... could she really? Could she find the same bravery she'd had last night before Gavin had rejected her? Granted, it hadn't been a harsh rejection, but it hadn't exactly made her eager to put herself out there again either. She didn't really want to hear 'I didn't come in here for that' or 'you're not ready for me' again.

"Um. A little embarrassed," she admitted. Gathering her bravery, she pushed herself up into a sitting position, brushing her hair back from her face. Was it her imagination, or had Alec just made a gargling sound? His eyes were now riveted to her exposed breasts—no, wait, he just looked up at, no never mind, back to her chest. Holding in a giggle, Kiara swayed. Just a little. Just to watch his eyes move back and forth with them.

Which they totally did.

She couldn't hold back her giggle then, it was too funny to watch his eyes following her nipples like he was hypnotized by them.

At her giggle, his eyes snapped up to her face, narrowing. Something almost predatory slid into his expression, fascinating her. Stags weren't predators—she certainly had more predator in her than he did—but suddenly she felt very much like prey.

"What are you doing, Kiara?" he asked, his voice deepening a little as he kept his eyes fixed on her face.

"Um... waiting to see what you're going to do?" She tried to make it come out cute, but the question sounded more vulnerable than anything else.

Setting his tablet down, eyes still trained on her, Alec sat up and leaned forward. Kiara swayed towards him, her weight coming down on her hands to meet him in the middle. He brushed his lips over hers, the touch lighter than a butterfly's wings.

"Well, I'm waiting to see what you want," he murmured, his lips brushed over her cheek, making her skin tingle and goosebumps stand up all over her body. "So why don't you tell me?"

"You," she whispered, mesmerized by the light touch of his mouth, yearning for more, emboldened by his movements and his question. "I want you... I want to...I want you inside me." She'd stumbled over the words, reaching for some that were graphic enough to state her intent but not so graphic she couldn't say them aloud. Once again, the romance novels she'd read had come to her rescue.

It was the right thing to say.

With a groan, Alec pressed his lips to hers, this time in a real kiss and Kiara reached up to wrap her hand around his neck and pull him down atop her. Her doe purred in approval, urging her more quietly than she had before, as if afraid to scare Kiara off again.

Unlikely at this point. Kiara's entire body felt like it was throbbing with need and she ached to be filled. To have him inside of her.

The weight of a hard, male body on hers made her moan, and his tongue slid into her mouth. He felt so good. Squirming beneath him, it didn't take much to coax him into the position she really wanted.

On her back with him settled over the length of her body, between her legs, the bulge of his jeans rubbing against her pussy. Fingers sliding into her hair as he kissed her, deeply and desperately, passionately but also gently.

"Oh Kiara, what are we going to do with you?" Gavin's amused question from the doorway had both her and Alec jerking in surprise.

Alec lifted his head to give his cousin a lazy smile, while Kiara battled with the sudden guilt of having been in a very similar position with Gavin this morning and now he was seeing her like this with Alec... but he was smiling.

"You could come over here and help me make our girl feel really, really good," Alec said. His hips moved, pressing against Kiara's core and making her gasp. She clung to his shoulders, trembling with both physical need and apprehensive excitement at what he was implying. "Unless you don't think you can handle that."

"Did you ask Kiara what she thinks about that?" Gavin asked, sounding a little exasperated as he sauntered forward. Kiara noticed he didn't shut the door behind him either. Did that mean Riley and Dorian might walk in at any time too?

Her doe purred harder.

The purring was odd but also soothing and encouraging. Even if *she* wasn't sure she could handle four men, her doe certainly seemed confident.

Both men were now looking at her, she realized. Blinking, she looked back at them.

"Think about what?" she asked, belatedly, genuinely confused as to what Gavin had meant.

Gavin halted at the edge of the bed, cocking his head at her. "Me joining you two in bed."

Oh. *Oh.* Her body clenched. Both of them? In bed with her at the same time? Touching her? Kiara's chest tightened and her pussy creamed. Her doe was practically crooning. There had been whispers about some of the does doing that with their mates, but Kiara never had. She hadn't wanted to even think about Sebastian with other females, much less be party to it happening.

But for some reason neither Alec nor Gavin seemed upset. Gavin looked envious of Alec, but not like he was seething with jealousy, the way Kiara would have been. If they were fine with the situation, why shouldn't she be?

"Yes, please," she said, feeling very shy.

The grin that lit up Gavin's entire face made her feel very, very good about her answer.

The next thing she knew, Gavin was on the bed with them, taking over kissing her mouth while Alec began kissing his way down her body. Kiara whimpered, mewling against Gavin's lips as Alec's mouth traveled over her neck, her collarbone, down to her breasts to suckle at her nipples.

She was on fire, her sensitive buds throbbing as Alec nibbled and sucked them, and her lower body bucked, trying to find more contact for her pussy. The needy ache to be filled was overwhelming her. With one hand on the back of Alec's head and the other wrapped in Gavin's hair, she already felt completely, wildly, erotically out of control.

When Alec reached her pussy with his mouth, spreading her thighs wide so he could slide his tongue between her swollen lips, Kiara screamed. Gavin swallowed the sound, one of his hands coming up to caress her breasts and she was overwhelmed with the sensations as the two men worked together. It only took a few flicks of Alec's tongue before she was writhing, practically sobbing with the ecstasy flowing through her.

Her body had been so primed, so hot for them, she'd cum with barely a touch to her clit.

"Oh... oh my goodness... oh my..." she said, panting, when Gavin lifted his lips from hers. Her fingers were still entwined in both of their hair, her body quivering from the intense pleasure. "That was amazing..."

Looking smug, Alec straightened somewhat, forcing her to release her grip on his hair. Reluctantly, she did the same with Gavin as Alec loomed over her. "You taste delicious, gorgeous."

"I do?" The surprise in her voice made both men pause in their movements—which was really a shame because Gavin was midway through pulling off his shirt and revealing more of his spectacular body again.

"Yeah, baby, you taste amazing," Alec said slowly. "No one's ever told you that before?"

"No one's ever done that before," Kiara said, pleased at the compliment. Then she shrank a little as both men exchanged one of their looks. A displeased one. Had she done something wrong?

Seeing her flinch, they both immediately turned to her, their expressions softening.

"It's okay, sweetheart," Gavin said soothingly, yanking his shirt the rest of the way off and dropping it on the bed. "We're not mad at you. We're mad *for* you. Oral pleasure is definitely not something you should have been deprived of."

"Well I didn't know about it, so I wasn't really deprived," she said matter-of-factly. "You can only be deprived of something if you know you're missing it." Which was true. She certainly hadn't felt deprived of a man's mouth between her legs before this. Although if she never had it ever again, she certainly would feel very deprived.

"You, gorgeous, are fucking amazing," Alec said, drawing her attention so she looked down the length of her body at him. He'd already stripped off all of his clothes and Kiara's eyes went wide at the sight of his naked body. Hard, lean muscles, a nice furry chest that trailed down the center of his stomach to the curls surrounding a very swollen, very nice cock. Thick, long, and dark pink, it looked like it was reaching for her.

Leaning forward, he kissed her mound, just above her own dark curls, and then began working his way back up her body. She was torn between watching Alec's slow approach as he retraced the path he'd made earlier or watching Gavin as he finished undressing.

Good mates, thought her doe approvingly.

Chapter 6

Feeling Kiara's body stiffen underneath his lips, Alec lifted his head again. He felt super-sensitive to her responses, wanting to make sure they didn't inadvertently push her into anything she wasn't ready for or misinterpret any signals she was sending.

"What's wrong, gorgeous?" he asked. His stag was impatient but also willing to wait, not wanting to accidentally drive their shy mate away. If she wanted to stop right now, he would. No matter how much his cock ached.

"I..." Her eyes darted between him and Gavin, who had just finished pulling his pants off but was now frozen, waiting for the verdict. "I'm not sure I should say..."

"Why not?" He was confused, but that wasn't a new emotion when it came to Kiara. Really, he'd expected a little bit of hesitation over including Gavin in the bedroom—many women did hesitate. There were a lot of societal hang-ups about a woman who slept with two men, much less four. Instead, Kiara had surprised him by not seeming to have a problem with the idea at all. He had some suspicions about why she wouldn't find more than two people in a bed together to be strange, but he didn't want to ask.

"I don't want you to stop," she said, a little miserably.

Alec choked back a laugh that threatened to bubble up in the back of his throat. She looked so worried, but the idea was ludicrous. Here she was, finally laid out naked beneath him, with her rounded breasts and pink-brown nipples tempting him to touch and lick, the taste of her honey still on his tongue, wet and ready for him, his stag riding him to fully claim her, and she really thought he might change his mind?

"Baby, the only thing that's going to make me want to stop is if *you* want to stop. Because if you're not into it, then I'm not into it, but that is literally the only reason."

Her eyes flitted back and forth between him and Gavin again, and Gavin nodded, backing him up.

"You should probably tell us," Gavin said seriously. "Otherwise Alec might cry."

"I could definitely scrounge up a tear or two if that would help," he said cheerfully, winking at her. Then he sniffled. Kiara giggled, just as they had intended.

She still looked worried, but the teasing had obviously helped her gather her courage.

"My doe thinks you're her mates," she whispered softly, averting her gaze as if afraid to see his or Gavin's expressions.

Staring down at her, Alec was dumbfounded. He could sense Gavin was equally at a loss. Fortunately, before the silence could stretch on for too long, his stag nudged him.

Say something! The order from his deer jolted in his head, followed by a mental mutter that felt suspiciously like *stupid human*.

"Well, yeah..." he said, and then wanted to wince because seriously, could he have less game? Oh, right, of course he could. He could be Gavin.

"Oh, sweetheart," Gavin said, leaning over to kiss Kiara's cheek, which resulted in her looking up towards him so he could kiss her lips. Dammit. Gavin might be winning in the game department currently, but Alec knew he could catch up and surpass his cousin. He just needed a second to get himself together. "Our stags want you as a mate, too."

"They do? Even Riley and Dorian?" She was so adorably surprised, it was all Alec could do to keep himself from kissing her senseless. And then plunging his cock inside of her and riding her to a screaming orgasm. *Her* screaming orgasm, specifically, although he doubted he'd be able to remain very quiet either.

"All of us," Alec confirmed, running his hands up her sides comfortingly, and enjoying the way she squirmed, her face lighting up at both his words and his touch.

"I'm the only one who came upstairs because we don't want to overwhelm you," Gavin explained. "Trust me, they want their turn with you as well."

"A little overwhelming is good," Alec said, leaning down to kiss her gorgeous breasts again. The perfect handful, he could spend all day on her breasts. "Don't you think so, Kiara?" He pinched her nipple, making her squeak and wriggle, her back arching slightly to press her chest up towards him. Delicious.

"Oh yes..."

And they were back in business.

******

Not really knowing what to expect, Kiara was still surprised when Alec settled between her legs, sliding his cock up and down her wet lips to tease her, while Gavin simultaneously took her hand and wrapped it around his cock. She hadn't really known what to do with both of them, so she was glad they took the lead. Dr. Tran had reassured them that they'd all know when she was in heat; the tinkering with her genetics wouldn't have changed that. So there was no danger there.

She was even gladder when Alec's cock began to press into her, stretching her muscles open as he thrust forward with a deep groan. Her fingers tightened around Gavin's cock, making him groan and thrust as well, so that her hand pumped his shaft. The combined movements of both men aroused her even more, despite her previous orgasm.

"Oh fuck..." Alec groaned as he moved his hips back and thrust forward again, making her writhe as he pressed deeper inside of her, filling her so wonderfully she thought she might climax again just from having him enter her. Her hand moved on Gavin's dick almost of its own volition, her own sexual excitement making her want to pump harder, to feel him throbbing against her palm.

"Yeeeeess...." The word hissed out of her as Alec buried himself inside of her, filling her completely, and her back arched as she ground her sensitive pussy lips against his groin.

Gavin began to fondle her breasts, adding to the sensations sweeping through her as Alec grasped one of her legs in each arm, holding her fully open as he began to move in and out of her clenching pussy, a look of total erotic bliss on his face. Her doe was exulting in being mounted by one of their mates, urging Kiara on, making her want to scratch and bite at both of the men, to mark them up and warn all other females away.

"Fuck... Gavin... she feels so fucking good..."

Hearing Alec talking about her to his cousin, the other man who was there with them in bed, made Kiara feel almost crazed with need. It was incredibly hot. She didn't at all regret not joining in with whatever Sebastian's other mates might have done with him. She wasn't turned on by having multiple people in bed with her, she was excited by their focus on *her*. She was greedy for their touch, for their pleasure, and she didn't want to share. They were hers.

All hers.

The hand not on Gavin's cock raked down the front of Alec's chest, her nails digging in and leaving five lines of red across his muscles. Alec threw back his head, crying out as he began to move harder, faster, making her sob as her sensitive tissues were stroked and stimulated. He hunched forward, pounding between her legs, surrounding her with his scent... but it was changing. He didn't just smell like himself anymore, he smelled like her too. Like their very essences were twining together as he moved inside of her.

The scent was strongest at the base of his neck, the crook of his shoulder, and Kiara had the unsettling sensation of her teeth feeling like they were lengthening.

Mine! Her doe's mental voice was full of possessive demand, her determined push too strong to ignore, and Kiara found herself sinking her teeth into Alec's flesh.

He screamed, a surprised howl of ecstatic incredulity, and Kiara found herself screaming too as he swelled up inside of her. At some point she had let go of Gavin's cock and now she was clinging to Alec for all she was worth, digging furrows into his back with her nails as she throbbed and pulsed around him, her fluttering muscles milking the cum from him until he was slumped over on top of her panting.

Only then did her fangs recede and Kiara dropped her head down on the mattress, her pussy still spasming around his softening cock. "Oh I'm sorry... I'm so sorry... I have no idea what just happened..."

"Holy shit..." Gavin breathed out the words as he stared wide eyed at his cousin. Alec was touching the already healing mark—although to Kiara's horror, she could see it wasn't healing exactly the way it was supposed to. Shifters healed at an advanced rate compared to humans and, unless silver was used to injure them, they healed without a scar. Except the bite mark on Alec's neck was definitely turning into a real mark. Her doe was smug and completely ignoring Kiara's internal admonishments. "She mate-marked you!"

"I what?" Kiara asked, distracted from scolding her unapologetic doe. "What is that?"

"It must be the jaguar in you coming out," Alec said, a sudden grin spreading across his face as he touched the spot with exploratory fingers. "I have a freaking mate mark!"

Well at least he didn't seem upset about it at all. A mate mark—now she remembered Jesse showing off hers back at Lakewood. Jesse had said deer didn't do that, but apparently jaguars did... at least Alec was enthusiastic about it, because Kiara didn't think she could take it back. Strangely, she had the oddest awareness of feeling Alec's excitement in her own head. She couldn't really ponder the sensation because a moment later, Kiara found herself being tugged out from under Alec's body and into position above Gavin's, straddling his hips as he looked up at her with an awed expression on his face.

"I want one," he demanded, his hands coming up to cup and squeeze her breasts. She was resting with the length of his cock along her sensitive folds, making her squirm against the steely ridge. Kiara shivered as he plucked at her nipples. After two orgasms she wasn't sure she could find a third one in her. Had she ever had two orgasms in such close proximity to each other before? If she had, she couldn't remember, but his hands on her breasts made her want to try for three. Inside her head, her doe was already pushing at her again, eager to mark and claim another of her mates.

"I'm not sure I have a choice about it," she admitted, already feeling the pressure from her doe to mount him and sink her teeth into him, not to mention claw him a little bit just to be sure it was clear who he belonged to. "I'm pretty sure if we have sex, my doe is going to insist on it."

Gavin grinned up at her, rolling her nipples between his fingers in a manner that made her gasp and rock on top of his erection, feeling it slide between her now ultra-slippery folds. Beside them, Alec was on his side, still stroking his own mark, watching them with a little light in his eyes.

"Better make sure you do, or he really will cry with envy," Alec teased, preening a little as he lengthened his neck, making sure to flash the mark at Gavin.

Ignoring his cousin, Gavin kept his focus on her, renewing her arousal as he continued to play with her breasts. "My stag is insisting on it too, beautiful, so please don't hesitate. I want you to ride me and claim me."

Well when he put it that way...

Kiara lifted herself up to position his erect cock at her entrance. After two orgasms, she felt exquisitely sensitive, her channel tighter than ever—or maybe that was just the position making her muscles tenser—as she began to work herself down onto him. Gavin groaned, moving beneath her and thrusting up into her, his hands sliding down to her waist.

Almost as soon as Gavin had readjusted his grip, Alec was kneeling half-beside and half-behind her, his front against her back as he cupped her breasts. Having both of their hands on her like this as she sank down onto Gavin's cock was a shockingly heady pleasure. The slickness of her pussy helped as she took him fully into her.

Caught between the two men, Kiara writhed on Gavin's cock, her muscles convulsing as she ground down atop him.

"Kiara!" He gasped out her name, his fingers digging into the soft flesh of her hips as he arched beneath her, thrusting up into her wet heat.

"That's it Kiara, you look so hot riding him," Alec said in her ear, nibbling on the tender lobe as he continued to play with her breasts. Her nipples felt so swollen, so overstimulated, she could barely stand it and yet she didn't want him to stop either. "Make him feel as good as you made me feel."

From competitors to co-lovers, she didn't entirely understand the cousins' relationship, but she didn't care right now. They were making her feel so good.

She rose and fell over Gavin, riding him just like Alec told her to, both males and her doe urging her on as her orgasm began to climb again. Kiara found herself leaning forward toward Gavin, drawn in by the intoxicating scents intermingling between them, wanting to wreathe herself in them.

As her passion rose, physical pleasure rippling through her, her teeth lengthened. Just as she had with Alec, Kiara's doe surged forward at the penultimate moment.

Mine!

Kiara writhed on top of Gavin, Alec beside them watching, as Gavin shouted and bucked beneath her, his cock throbbing inside of her as he came in response to the mating bite.

Slumping on top of him, Alec moving in to nuzzle and stroke her back as she panted with exertion, Kiara couldn't remember ever having felt happier. Her doe was smugly satisfied inside her head, far more than she'd ever been with Sebastian. Both males were now stroking and cuddling her, murmuring their admiration of her.

Still, an anxious nervousness rose up inside her as well, even as her eyes closed sleepily. This couldn't really be her life, could it? Was she about to wake up and find it was a dream?

******

Not a dream. She woke up from her second nap of the day to the smell of something delicious, still wedged between Gavin and Alec's hard bodies. Waking up between two men was very nice, she decided. If they really were her mates, she was going to request they sleep like this. Although, her doe seemed to think Riley and Dorian were her mates as well, and so did Gavin and Alec. So how would that work?

Rubbing her nose in Gavin's chest hair, breathing in the sweet smell of their mingled scents, Kiara was feeling decidedly optimistic. They'd all make it work somehow.

Both Alec and Gavin woke up when she tried to slide out from between them. Smelling the same thing she did, it wasn't hard to convince them to get up, although both of them eyed her naked body in a promising way. She still felt a little shy in front of them, but not so much so that she tried to hide herself again.

They certainly weren't shy. Kiara took a little longer about cleaning herself up, but when she went downstairs she nearly burst into giggles upon seeing the younger brothers strutting around completely shirtless while their older brothers reacted in their own individual manner. Dorian was scowling at both Gavin and Alec, looking incredibly envious although he pretended to be completely focused on setting out dinner (the lasagna looked heavenly and smelled even better) while Riley was trying to get a better look at the marks.

"Do you think the scratches might be her jaguar presenting as well?" he asked, having successfully cornered Alec against some cabinets, poking the bite scar his brother now had and peering curiously at it.

"How would I know? Stop that!" Alec batted his older brother's hand away, looking increasingly mutinous. "I am not one of your science experiments. Get your own. Or go bother Gavin at least."

"Don't you dare," Gavin said, protectively covering his own mark and backing away as Riley turned his inquisitive gaze on the other man.

Lifting his head up from where he was setting the lasagna down in the center of the table, Dorian immediately spotted her standing at the base of the stairs, and his expression softened and filled with a kind of yearning. "Hey there, angel, how are you feeling? Hungry, I hope?"

The second question made her feel less prickly about the first. She was getting kind of tired of being constantly asked how she was. Unless she actually looked in distress, did she really have to keep telling them she was fine? But it seemed like Dorian was actually asking in general, not specifically about her recovery.

"Very hungry," she said, feeling a bit shy now that everyone was looking at her. Riley had the same kind of yearning in his eyes that Dorian did, while Alec and Gavin stared at her with a kind of awed possessiveness that her doe returned. Seeing the two unmarked men was riling up her animal. Kiara's lower body quivered a little, making her want to groan. Her body was insatiable. Was this an effect of her new genes or just meeting the men?

She kept asking herself that question about so many things in this new life of hers, but she had no idea if she'd ever receive any answers. There might not be any way to tell. So maybe she should just accept this turn of good fortune and stop trying to question everything about it... but she couldn't seem to stop. Some part of her kept waiting for something to come along and ruin everything. This felt too good, too surreal to continue forever.

Pushing her pessimism to the back of her mind, Kiara sat down for dinner and enjoyed another wonderful meal with the stags. As if by some unspoken agreement, Riley and Dorian sat on either side of her while Gavin and Alec sat on the other side of the table. She wondered if their stags were affecting their seating choices. Her doe was certainly pleased at having her two as-yet unclaimed mates right next to her. Not that the other side of the table was very far away or anything, but she was feeling even more possessive over the two she hadn't mate-marked yet.

Afterwards they watched a movie and, once again, Riley and Dorian claimed the spots on either side of her. As they watched the hero and heroine running from the bad guys, Kiara somehow ended up with her head on Dorian's thigh while he stroked her hair and her feet on Riley's lap as he gave them a massage. Her doe was purring in approval again, although she was also feeling somewhat impatient.

They all went upstairs together, and about five minutes after she'd gone to her own room, there was a knock on her door.

"Come in," she called, turning, her doe perking up with anticipation. They'd both been feeling just a tiny bit abandoned when all the men had gone to their own rooms. The door opened to reveal Riley, looking both awkward and sheepish as he came into her room. He was wearing pajama bottoms and a tank top, much as Gavin had the night before, and Kiara couldn't help but wonder if all the males slept that way.

"Ah... I don't want to be presumptuous, but I was hoping maybe we could talk before you go to bed and, ah, if things go well—" His voice cut off as Kiara bounded over and grabbed his face between her hands, pulling him down for a kiss.

Adorable male. Sweet mate. Because Riley was definitely the sweetest. He was so often in his own little world and he was definitely willing to tease his brothers, but his kindness and gentleness imbued his entire being. Where Alec and Gavin had strolled in, cocky and confident, Riley was worried she might think he was there for exactly the reason she wanted him there.

Once she was enthusiastically kissing him though, he obviously knew how to go on from there. Two large hands cupped her bottom and lifted her up so she could wrap her legs around his waist, feeling the ridge of his erection through the flannel pajama bottoms he was wearing. Even though she'd already had three orgasms today, she felt antsy and not quite fulfilled—maybe because her doe was so intent on claiming all of her mates? Maybe because, deep down, she'd been worried she was on her own for the night when they'd all gone back to their own rooms?

Riley didn't seem like he wanted to be anywhere else though. He was kissing her just as passionately, skillfully, and thoroughly as his brother and cousin had, carrying her over to the bed. Running her hands over his muscled shoulders, Kiara breathed in deeply, her doe's purring beginning again as she could tell their scents were already beginning to mingle. Just a little.

She wanted more.

They reached the bed and Kiara squeaked with delight as Riley ended the kiss so he could roll them onto the bed without letting her go. He was grinning, his hazel-green eyes glowing brightly with hot desire.

"You are very eager," he said. Kiara blinked in surprise, not really sure what to do with that statement. Seeing her confusion, he explained in earnest. "I'm not complaining. I just can't help but wonder if it's the urge to claim a mate or if your libido is just high."

"I don't know either," Kiara replied, relieved someone else was having the same thoughts she was. Finally! Someone to match her curiosity.

Thinking it over for a moment, Riley shrugged. "I think the only way to truly ascertain the answer is to have you claim each of us and then see if your urge to copulate decreases."

Both of them ignored the loud groan from the next room over—Alec's room—which was perfectly audible to their shifter hearing.

Kiara was delighted Riley's scientific brain brought up the same kinds of questions she asked herself and—more than that—that he actually suggested they could answer one of the questions plaguing her. Even better, the test involved what she desperately wanted to do anyway, what her doe was insisting she do. "That sounds like a *wonderful* idea."

To her simultaneous annoyance and delight, Riley did not get right down to business the way Alec and Gavin had. She wanted to go, go, go, and yet he took his time.

Explored her body.

Stroked her from the sensitive nape of her neck down her collarbone to her breasts, down her sides, around her hips, pressing his lips here and there as his fingers led the way.

Yes, she was being undressed, but so slowly... and yet she couldn't find it in herself to hurry him either, no matter how impatient her physical needs were making her feel.

Part of her was loving this intimate, thorough inspection of all her most sensitive spots, but the other part of her was ready to explode.

Just when she thought she might have to demand he fuck her, right now, Riley spread her legs apart and began another long, slow, thorough investigation. Using his tongue, he began to take a tour of her pussy, and both Kiara and her doe decided she could wait to demand he hurry it up. She moaned, her legs draped over his shoulders, hands in his hair, as he licked, nibbled, teased, and finally sucked her clit into his mouth, tonguing the sensitive nubbin while she screamed with utter ecstasy as her orgasm pounded through her.

The pleasure was so intense, she continued to throb even after he'd moved his mouth away from her pussy, looking highly pleased with himself.

"Oh my goodness..." she murmured, utterly limp. "That was amazing..."

"You are very sensitive," he said appreciatively, bracing himself on his elbows above her, the backs of his fingertips brushing against her cheeks. "I think I have determined your most—"

Kiara pulled him down for another kiss, interrupting him. As curious as she was, as satisfied as she was after that intense climax, she wasn't done with him yet and she definitely didn't want to become derailed by an explanation of where she was the most sensitive. She wanted to *feel* it.

The taste of her own pleasure on his lips was odd but not unarousing, especially because it heightened the way their scents mingled. She moaned as Riley's cock nudged against her pussy and then pressed inward, his hands moving towards those sensitive spots he'd located on her body to torment her some more as he began to fuck her.

Slowly.

Deeply.

Thoroughly.

It was heaven. It was exquisite torture.

Thankfully he'd already made her orgasm once or she'd be screaming with impatience. Instead, she was able to enjoy every second of his lingering thrusts, the way he experimented with his movements, grinding himself against her pussy, thrusting shallowly and then deeper, his hands moving up and down between her breasts and her hips. When he pressed one hand over her mound, his thumb slipping down between their bodies to rub against her clit, Kiara writhed as her pleasure mounted quickly.

He thrust a little faster, a little harder, his thumb working on her sensitive nubbin and Kiara arched, crying out as the first wave of her orgasm hit.

That was when Riley finally gave in to the urges of his body, no longer holding back. Kiara screamed as the waves of ecstasy intensified under the hard thrusts in and out of her body, her nails digging into his shoulders as she pulled his upper body down to clamp on to his shoulder. He yelled out hoarsely, bucking and surging inside of her as she gave him the mating bite, their combined ecstasy spiraling wildly out of control.

Wet heat pulsed inside of her as he came, and her doe purred in contentment.

One more mate claimed.

Panting, Riley slumped atop her as her fangs receded, turning back into normal human teeth.

"That was... that was... indescribable," he finally said in between panted breaths. "I don't even know how to analyze that. I don't know that it's possible."

A deep chuckle drew both of their attention as Dorian opened the door and came into the room, acting very much like he belonged there. Much more so than any of the other males had. His arrogant manner both ruffled Kiara's fur and appealed to her. Something else which she couldn't explain.

Shutting the door behind him, Dorian sauntered over to the bed, his dark eyes appreciatively taking in the tangle of naked limbs. A smile curled his lips. Unlike Riley, he was clothed only in a pair of boxers, which did nothing to hide his very large erection tenting the front. Completely unconcerned by his obvious arousal, he climbed into bed with them as Riley slid down on her opposite side.

Kiara was breathless, a little sore, but also eager to claim her last mate. Which was why she was very confused when Dorian pulled the covers up over all of them and reached out to turn off the lamp.

"What... Aren't you..." She was so confused she couldn't even think of how to ask the question.

"I'm going to sleep, and so are you two," Dorian said authoritatively. On her other side, Riley was already settling in facing her, his head on the pillow, and his hand on her soft belly. She couldn't help but pout a little, even if her pussy was getting a little sore and she'd already had five amazing orgasms today. Even her doe was feeling sulky, although she also seemed to realize Dorian was serious. "You need to rest."

She would have protested, but as soon as he said it, she had the irresistible urge to yawn.

Damn him. She covered up her mouth as she did so, scowling.

The light blinked out which meant he couldn't even see her glaring at him. Kiara pouted.

Hard hands cupped her face and hot lips covered hers.

Dorian didn't just kiss her. He possessed her mouth, claiming it with his tongue, and heating up her body all over again.

"I can feel you pouting, little girl," he said when he pulled away. A softer kiss was pressed against her forehead. "Go to sleep."

Two male bodies protectively curled around hers, trapping her between them. Still a bit put-out, Kiara sighed, but closed her eyes.

If Dorian thought she was going to be put off forever though, he was going to be sadly disappointed. Just like when she'd left her community, Kiara had made her decision, for better or worse. Now she was going to grab onto this opportunity with both hands—and if that meant latching onto him with her teeth when he least expected it, then so be it.

Chapter 7

Kiara woke up first. She knew she was the first awake because Dorian was snoring softly, and Riley's breathing was far too even and steady to be anything other than asleep.

Very carefully turning on to her side to face Dorian, Kiara examined his sleeping visage. He looked a lot softer in the morning light, his face missing its usual watchful and stern expression. The sheets had been pushed down at some point in the night, revealing his broad chest, sprinkled with dark, wiry hair. She had the most insane urge to rub her face all over those ridged muscles.

She was pretty certain that was her doe's impulse, wanting to stamp her claim on him with both scent and physical markers.

The only one of her mates still unbitten.

Licking her lips, Kiara reached out and very gently lifted the sheets, pulling it down so she could see the ridge of his erection pressing against his boxers. A very large erection. Letting the sheets drop on his thighs, she glanced at him. Eyes still closed. Still snoring softly. Face still relaxed.

She shoved her hand down his boxers and wrapped her fingers around the hot, thick rod of male flesh, staring at his face the entire time.

The moment her palm touched his cock, his eyelashes were opening, his eyes dark and stormy as she gripped him. Meeting her gaze, the corner of his mouth quirked up in a kind of cocky amusement.

"Good morning, naughty girl," he said, his voice an even deeper rumble than usual.

In one swift movement—Kiara couldn't quite see or understand how—she suddenly went from leaning up on her elbow next to him with her hand around his dick to being dragged over his lap as he sat up straight. Squeaking in surprise, she wriggled against his erection, while Dorian palmed her bottom, yanking down her pajama pants and panties to reveal her upturned bottom.

"What are you doing?!" Even her doe seemed to be in shock at this unexpected turn of events.

"Giving you a little taste of what naughty girls get."

SMACK!

Before she could protest, before she could question, his hard palm had come down on her bottom. The swat wasn't particularly painful—it stung and made her skin tingle a bit— but she shrieked anyway in both surprise and embarrassed outrage. Which did absolutely nothing to deter him.

SMACK!

"Ow! Let me up!"

"No." His tone was implacable and unapologetic.

SMACK!

The heat of each slap against her bottom made her squirm against him, uncomfortably aware that some part of her was actually enjoying being over his lap in this helpless position while he spanked her. She'd read one book where the heroine had been spanked and it had fired up her imagination when she'd been reading, but she hadn't realized Dorian—or any real live man for that matter—would actually do such a thing.

SMACK!

"Ow!"

Or that it would *sting* so much.

With her legs and upper body resting on the mattress she couldn't kick or fight him, especially not with one large palm pressing down in the center of her back and pinning her in place. She felt more than a little embarrassed even as she was helplessly aroused, and when she saw Riley watching them from the other side of the bed, his expression bemused, she reached out to him.

"Riley! Help me!"

Chuckling, Dorian didn't even pause.

SMACK! SMACK! SMACK!

"You appear to be enjoying yourself, Kiara. I would prefer not to deny both you and Dorian this pleasure," Riley replied, to her consternation.

"I am not!"

SMACK! SMACK!

Then Dorian rubbed her pinked bottom and Kiara moaned at the delicious sensations of her heated skin tingling under the rough squeezes of his hand.

"All evidence to the contrary," Riley said, amusement tinging his voice. Kiara opened one narrowed at him, glaring. He looked back at her, calmly. "I'm going to go get breakfast started. You two enjoy yourselves. Kiara, if you really want him to stop, he will, but I'm pretty sure you don't."

With that, Riley got up (ignoring his own massive and obvious erection) and exited, leaving her to Dorian's tender mercies. Narrowing her eyes, she looked over her shoulder at the big alpha male, daring him to swat her again.

SMACK!

Chuckling at her shriek of outrage, Dorian picked her up and tossed her onto the bed. Somehow, he managed to yank her pants and panties the rest of the way off of her at the same time. Kiara didn't know whether to be impressed or even more miffed at him. Bouncing on the bed just made her even more aware of the newly ultra-sensitive skin on her bottom, and she would have scrambled away, just to make him chase her a little more, but he was too fast.

His muscled body wedged between her legs, his weight resting on her lower body and making her pussy throb, while his hands gripped her wrists, holding them above her head.

Kiara froze, the prey instincts of her deer taking over as his dark eyes glittered down hotly at her.

"Well, bad girl, what do you have to say for yourself?" he asked, rocking himself against her body and making her ache to have him actually inside of her. The movement made her bottom tingle as her skin was rubbed against the bedsheets beneath her and she pouted up at him.

"I didn't say you could spank me!"

"And I didn't say you could put your hand on my cock."

"You liked it!"

"You liked the spanking," he countered, leaning forward to give her nose a little kiss, making her bite back a moan as the movement increased the exquisite pressure on her swollen clit. "Your pussy is soaking the front of my boxers right now. I think you wanted to see what would happen and now you know... I think you liked being a naughty... little... girl..." He thrust his hips in time with his last three words, and Kiara writhed against his hard erection, sliding between her plump lips.

Her doe was of no help either. The predatory animal had gone all soft and submissive under Dorian's sensual assault, just like Kiara had.

Being unable to reach up and touch him was as exciting as it was frustrating, and she found she was enjoying his particular brand of dominant-love making just as she had Alec and Gavin's paired erotic assault and Riley's thorough sensuality.

******

Dorian could tell the moment Kiara and her doe submitted to him, softening beneath him. His stag chuffed with satisfaction, eager to claim her and be bitten by her in turn now that they'd established who was in actually in charge.

She was a sassy, playful little thing, completely into what they were doing, and he was enjoying her uninhibited, natural responses to his dominance. Although he didn't think she was fully submissive sexually, she would be for him—and then she could work out her other desires on his brother and cousins.

Transferring hold of her wrists to one hand, he used the other to tug her shirt off over her head. Her wide dark eyes stared up at him, shiny with excitement and anticipation. Dorian made a mental note to definitely try some cuffs or ropes with her sometime; he had a feeling she would very much enjoy it.

"Are you going to let my hands go?" she asked, a little breathlessly, sounding uncertain about what she wanted the answer to be, as if her thoughts were traveling along a similar path as his.

"I don't think I am, no," he said, grinning as he leaned down to suck one pert nipple into his mouth. Kiara whimpered, arching, making him press down more firmly on her wrists with the hand gripping them. She practically quivered with excitement when his hold didn't yield, keeping her trapped in place.

Now he used his free hand to peel his boxers off, switching his oral attentions between her swollen nipples, teasing her, dominating her, and readying himself to claim her. The sweet musk of her pussy filled the air as he aroused her, and he could identify the rest of his herd in her scent. Soon his own essence would join them, and they'd be complete.

His stag prodded him in urgent approval, wanting soon to be *right now*.

Kissing his way up her breasts to her collarbone and then up her neck, Dorian pressed the head of his cock to her slick opening and pushed in. They both moaned together as her wet heat caressed his length, stretching around him and tightening pleasurably.

"Oh yes..." She planted her feet on the bed, pushing upwards to take more of him inside of her and Dorian groaned with appreciation.

Little minx. He amended his mental note about the cuffs to include some for her ankles too. Of course, just thinking about her completely bound and helpless beneath him as he teased her mercilessly and took his time only increased his need to fill her, fuck her, claim her.

Ours... give her our scent... His stag urged, desperate to be included in the changes her scent had already gone through.

Pressing his lips to hers, Dorian felt her whimper as he began to thrust, hard.

******

Oh. My. Goodness.

Dorian had not been kidding when he said he was rough. His cock was just as large as the others, but he didn't go slow, he didn't take his time, he didn't work himself into her. Instead he filled her, hard and fast, dominating her, taking her for a ride she was unable to control. Whatever stinging her bottom had felt was gone now, the sensation mingling into her pleasure so thoroughly she couldn't tell if her skin even hurt anymore.

She was on fire with need, inside and out, her doe even more riled up because he was the last of her mates, the final piece to her puzzle, and she was feeling desperate for both her orgasm and to mark him. A desperation which was further fueled by being pinned down on the bed beneath him, unable to claw him up the way her jaguar side desperately wanted to. Kiara was sure it was her jaguar because her doe would never even think about having, much less using, claws.

Straining against him only made her feel even more vulnerable as he easily held her arms in place with one hand, using his arm to wrap under her leg and slide her knee into the crook of his elbow. The position opened her body further to him, splaying her pussy open so his hard thrusts slammed against her sensitive lips and clit, making her sob with growing sexual rapture as she tried again to reach for him.

Again, she couldn't move her arms even a centimeter.

"Please!"

If anything, her plea made Dorian move harder, faster.

"Please, what, little girl?" he growled, bending her practically in half as he pounded into her, filling her over and over, heating her insides with the hard friction of his deep strokes.

"I need to touch you."

He groaned, held her for a moment longer, and then released her wrists.

Being freed had an immediate effect on both Kiara and her doe—it was as if all the need she'd been forced to keep down hit her and sent her into a frenzy. Dorian cried out hoarsely as her nails and teeth sank in, thrusting hard and fast as they both fell into a torrent of ecstatic bliss.

Mine! The thought ran in Kiara's head, filled with triumph through the hot waves of her orgasm.

******

"Holy hell! What did she do to you?" Alec asked, sounding awed as Dorian strutted into the kitchen, completely shirtless despite Kiara's best efforts to try to talk him into wearing one.

Frenzy had definitely been the right word to describe the state he'd driven her doe to. His upper body was covered with scratches from her nails; they scored his shoulders, back, and chest. They were healing, as shifters did, but the red lines were still clearly visible and probably would be for the next few hours.

Feeling both mortified and smug, Kiara followed him into the room, blushing and averting her gaze. She shouldn't have worried. The other males were far too interested in inspecting how much damage she'd done to their leader.

Gavin let out a low whistle. "Damn. I mean, I thought what you two were doing sounded hot but... damn."

"I want to watch next time," Alec said grinning, turning towards Kiara and catching her eye so he could wink at her. "If that's okay with you, sweetheart."

"Um, I guess so?" she said, although it came out more as a question. Blushing, she picked up one of the plates of eggs, bacon, and toast Riley had left on the counter, so he could go inspect Dorian's sex wounds. The idea of being watched definitely wasn't a turn off so she didn't object, but she also didn't really know what was considered 'normal' either. Now that her doe wasn't driving her with an implacable desire to mate and claim the men she felt a lot more awkward.

Although still horny as she looked them all over, especially when she thought about them watching her in bed with each other. So apparently her doe hadn't been responsible for everything.

Before she had even made it to the table, all four men were surrounding her, reaching out to touch and soothe her.

"Whatever you're comfortable with."

"We don't have to watch."

"We can take turns if you want."

Kiara couldn't help but start giggling, they were so adorably concerned—not to mention sexy as all heck and they definitely hadn't understood why she had sounded so hesitant.

"Really?" She couldn't help but tease them, looking up at Dorian with wide eyes. "What if I'm not comfortable being spanked anymore?"

All of them relaxed at her tone, realizing they had misinterpreted and that she was just fine.

Leaning over, Dorian whispered in her ear, sending little shivers up and down her spine. "You'd be lying, little girl. Which is very naughty, and you already know what happens to naughty girls."

Making a little 'eep' noise, still giggling, Kiara broke free of their little huddle and headed to the table with her breakfast. It only took a few moments for the men to join her—and immediately there was some jostling for who was going to sit next to her. Dorian didn't jockey for position. He sat down across from her, still grinning smugly, as the other three tried to push each other out of the way. She ended up with Riley on one side, Alec on the other, and both twins across on the other side of the table.

After that she felt much more natural. It was like nothing had really changed except that she didn't feel as unsure of herself anymore. They each wore her mark, proudly and where it was visible even though everyone except Dorian was wearing a shirt. Not a single one of them had a collar covering up his mate mark.

Gavin took her for a run after eating, to show her his favorite spot in the forest, a little nook under a tree where he'd made a kind of nest. When they returned Kiara spent some time with Riley in the garage, learning about the project he'd been tinkering with. He was building some kind of "battle robot" as he called it for a club he was in with some of the other soldiers at Lakewood.

She was helping Alec put lunch together when Dorian came into the room, cell phone in hand and a serious expression on his face. "Kiara. Dr. Tran is on the phone for you."

"For me?" Startled, she held out her hand to take the phone as Dorian and Alec exchanged one of their looks. Lifting the phone to her ear, she did her best to ignore them. "Hello?"

"Hello, Kiara, I'm so sorry to bother you, we're having a bit of an incident here at Lakewood. A Pudu deer shifter who says his name is Sebastian is here, demanding he see you and kicking up quite a fuss about us kidnapping and running experiments on his mate. Is there any way you could come back here this afternoon to help clear this up?"

Kiara dropped the phone from nerveless fingers, her heart racing as fear clogged her throat.

He's found me.

He's come to take me back.

No! Her deer was fierce in her rejection. *Not going! Staying here with mates!*

She was so trapped in immediate panic that she didn't even notice Alec had caught the phone until she heard him speaking to Dr. Tran.

"Hi Dr. Tran, it's Alec Walker. We're about to eat lunch but we'll head over right after," Alec said calmly. Obviously, he'd overheard everything the doctor had said. With shifter hearing it wasn't exactly hard to hear an entire phone conversation.

Shocked, Kiara stared at him, her eyes going wider as her heart sank into her stomach. Seeing her expression, Alec frowned at her.

"Don't look at me like that, beautiful," he said. "You can't possibly think we're going to let you go anywhere now."

"Definitely not," Dorian said, stretching out his arms and cracking his neck from side to side. "On the contrary, I am very much looking forward to meeting your ex and having a few words."

That was when it finally hit home for her—she wasn't alone anymore. She wouldn't have to face Sebastian alone, she was no longer powerless or completely ignorant to what the rest of the world held, and she didn't have to go back.

And you have me. Her doe bared her very sharp teeth.

All of the sudden Kiara was rather looking forward to seeing Sebastian too.

******

All of the men came with her, although by the time Gavin and Riley were told what was going on she wasn't surprised when they immediately declared they were going to be there too.

Still, the closer the car came to Lakewood, the more her anxieties began to rise. She was still in her human form, and she'd run from him after he'd beaten her while she was human. Her doe hadn't been able to do anything but help her heal. Of course the men were with her now, so she didn't need to fear Sebastian's violence, but...

He could be so convincing. There was a reason he had become one of the leaders of the community, even at his younger age in comparison with the rest of the elders. Sebastian had a charisma and charm innate to his person.

Was it possible he could convince the people at Lakewood that he really was her mate? Yes, she wanted to be with her herd, but was it possible they could be separated from her? After all, Dr. Tran had already requested Kiara come to help straighten things out with Sebastian. Which meant people were already listening to him.

Had been listening to him while she'd been eating lunch.

"Calm down, gorgeous," Gavin murmured in her ear. "I can feel your anxiety. It's all going to be okay."

Startled, she blinked, turning her head to him. "You can feel my anxiety?"

"Of course, sweetheart, we're mates," he said with a cocky grin, leaning over to plant a kiss on her forehead. "You can feel us too. Just think about it."

Staring at him for a moment, she closed her eyes, prodding inside of her head.

Sure enough, there were four little spots of calm emanating from somewhere in her head. It was kind of like having her doe in her head, but different. The four spots were separate from her and yet they could affect her. No wonder she'd been so calm during lunch.

"You can do this," Riley said from the other side of her. His hand was resting on her thigh. "We will not abandon you. Ever."

Dorian parked the car in front of the hospital. Everything looked totally normal, there was no angry ex-mate waiting outside of the doors, no condemning group gathered to glare at her, nothing out of the ordinary.

Both he and Alec turned around to look at her, sitting between Gavin and Riley.

"You can do this, sweetheart," Alec said gently. "We've got you."

Giving her a once over, Dorian nodded his head. "Are you ready?"

Taking a deep breath, Kiara gathered her courage. Her doe curled her metaphorical lip in a sneer, flashing fang.

"Let's do this."

Chapter 8

Walking into the main entrance of Lakewood's hospital, Kiara was surprisingly close to having a giggling fit. Her mates had spread themselves around her like a phalanx of guards, two in front of her, two behind her. They were so much larger than her she could barely see any of the other people when trying to peer past Dorian and Riley's broad shoulders.

She was definitely still feeling nervous, but most of her anxiety had been soothed by the men and their possessive, protective stances. It was clear that they weren't going to give her up to anyone without a fight.

Hopefully it wouldn't come to that though.

The idea that it might was mostly what had her nerves on edge.

"Kiara? Kiara, honey, is that you?" Sebastian's smooth, concerned voice grated over those same nerves like nails on a chalkboard, making her wince. She could just barely see him coming toward her through the tiny space between Riley and Dorian's arms. "Oh, thank God you're okay."

Confused, Kiara stopped walking, jerking back and slamming into Gavin—thankfully he caught her before she could tip over completely. Dorian and Riley both glanced over their shoulders to see what was going on, but Dorian quickly turned back to face Sebastian, holding up his hand to indicate the other man should halt.

Looking both worried and confused, Sebastian stopped moving a few feet away from Dorian and Riley trying to peer past them. Everyone in the hospital lobby was now looking at them curiously, more than one of the women blatantly checking out all five of the men. With his dark, curling hair sprinkled with just a bit of grey, soulful brown eyes, and tanned skin, Sebastian was just as physically attractive as any of the other men. He wasn't attractive to her anymore though, not now that she'd glimpsed beneath the mask.

"Who are you?" he asked Dorian. "Why are you keeping me from my mate?"

Immediately the tension in the air heightened, all four of her males shifting their postures from defensive to ready-to-attack.

"She's not your mate," Dorian growled back at Sebastian.

"Of course she is," Sebastian said, drawing himself up to his full height, his dark eyes flashing dangerously. Kiara clung to Gavin, feeling a bit like cowering as she recognized the stance. Both he and Alec pressed in on either side of her, making soft soothing noises. "Kiara, step away from those men."

"No, she's going to stay right where she is," Riley said calmly but implacably. "You're not getting anywhere near her until you explain to *us* why you're here." Looking at him, Sebastian seemed to recognize the other man wasn't going to be moved by passionate emotion. He looked around at the four men and their implacable faces and came to some kind of conclusion, but Kiara wasn't sure what. Immediately his own posture changed, his demeanor shifting—Sebastian at his most genial, his most convincing.

Kiara found herself holding her breath, waiting to see what he would say, what claim he thought he could make. Especially since he didn't even know who these men guarding her were.

"I'm here to collect my mate," Sebastian said somberly, the very picture of an earnest, caring man just trying to do the right thing. "She's... well, her *health* is rather delicate. She's quite harmless but she does occasionally put herself in rather dangerous situations. We're in the middle of getting her help, but she didn't want to take her medications and..."

He spread his hands helplessly as cold fury washed through Kiara. Seriously? He was implying she was mentally unstable? Her doe snorted in fury, snarling with all the fury of a provoked jaguar.

Granted, she was a little different from the rest of the Pudu females—always had been—but that didn't make her *crazy!*

"How *dare* you?!" she shrieked, trying to dive forward, between Riley and Dorian, at him. Gavin caught her again, but this time he was holding her back rather than keeping her from falling over. "I am not mentally disturbed, and I do not need medication!"

"You see?" Sebastian said, ignoring her completely and appealing to the men in front of her, making her even more furious. She wanted to pound the falsely sincere expression off of his face. "She flies off the handle at even the mention of her illness. I don't believe she would hurt anyone..." But he made it sound as though he was uncertain of that statement. "As her mate, she's my responsibility. I can take over her care from here, she won't bother you again, you can be sure of that."

Kiara had thought she couldn't get any angrier, although she also realized her rage was at least partially driven by fear as well.

Fear that Sebastian would be believed.

Fear that her herd would turn away from her.

But even through that fear, she suddenly felt something else too.

Righteous indignation and anger—on her behalf.

Utter disbelief—aimed at Sebastian.

Love—directed at her.

Emotions pulsing through the bond between her and her herd, and she realized she didn't need to worry about them believing a word of Sebastian's lies. She didn't need to worry about their reactions.

She could already feel them.

Straightening up, she leaned against Gavin's side, enjoying the startled expression on Sebastian's face as he took in her abrupt change in demeanor as well as the falsely sweet smile on her face.

"I'm not your mate," she said, calmly and confidently. "And I'm definitely not going anywhere with you."

"Sorry man," Gavin said, grinning widely, but only his lips were smiling. His eyes were glaring at Sebastian, hard and unfriendly. In front of her Dorian and Riley didn't move an inch, just stood there staring at Sebastian in imperious silence. "But the lady has spoken."

The other three men nodded. Dorian crossed his arms over his chest and even though Kiara couldn't see his expression, she could practically feel the menace coming off of him. Or maybe that was just the mate bond, because Sebastian didn't seem to be affected by Dorian's intimidating posture.

"It doesn't matter what *she* says!" Sebastian looked outraged, shocked out of his charming persona by the—as he saw it—outrageous statement. "What kind of men are you that you would allow her to dictate your actions? Are you weak? Stupid?"

The sound of cloth ripping, and a large cat's snarl interrupted his tirade as Kiara threw herself forward. Her deer might be small but her now-very-dense muscles easily shredded the thin fabric of the shirt she was wearing as she shifted.

Everything seemed to happen in slow motion then. Alec and Gavin both yelping in surprise, Gavin holding up the shreds of her shirt, as Dorian and Riley turned to see what had happened. Sebastian's eyes growing wide with shock as he got a look at her new doe form.

"What the hell is wrong with her teeth?!" he shrieked, voice high with fear. "Why does she sound like that?"

Now he was the one afraid.

And his fear smelled delicious.

Her doe snarled again, the sound loud and unnatural, and launched forward between Dorian and Riley. They both tried to catch her, but she was so small, and they were so large they ended up just getting in each other's way and missing her entirely. Sebastian had already turned tail and taken off down the hallway, sprinting away from her tiny, vicious doe. A few muffled shouts of laughter followed them, which she ignored.

Later she would remember and realize how insanely ludicrous they must have looked—a tall, muscular dark-haired man running away from a miniature doe (even if she did have jaguar teeth), but as it was happening all she could think about was wanting to get some of her own back.

Wanting him to know how he'd made her feel.

Unfortunately, deer hooves were not meant for running on linoleum floors and it was obvious Sebastian was much faster than her as he pelted down the hallways yelling for help.

As he passed one doorway, it opened, and what looked like a person was stepping out, and suddenly a massive, white fluffy ball of fur filled the hallway and blocked Kiara from her prey.

What the heck is that?! Kiara thought as she frantically tried to skid to a halt. She just barely managed to keep from crashing into the thing when it turned its big head and she saw the huge pink twitchy nose and long white ears. *Holy... that is one big bunny.*

It was also between her and her prey.

Her doe yowled, showing her teeth, hunching back as if to spring.

The bunny growled back, the noise just as unnatural and strange as the ones Kiara made. It didn't just smell like rabbit, it smelled like bear and something reptilian.

Its teeth were also very sharp and a lot bigger than Kiara's doe's.

Defeated, she sat down on her haunches as the pounding footsteps behind her finally caught up. She let out a little huff of surprise as a strong arm curved around her body and lifted her up by her midsection, leaving her feet hanging down. Swinging her head around, she wasn't even a little surprised to see it was Dorian now holding her. He wasn't looking at her though, he was looking at the bunny.

"I know you're not Brady, Brock, or Brice," he said, tilting his head. "But you're bear sized, which means you must be Bethany."

Kiara blinked. That was a lot of names started with the letter 'B'. And they were all monster bunnies? That was just ludicrous.

"Yes, she is," said a stern voice from the other side of her. "Shift back, Bethany."

The bunny made a chuffing sound, but a moment later a gorgeous, completely naked, petite blonde stood in front of Kiara in its place. Behind the woman a very tall, very scary looking man had Sebastian by the scruff of his neck. With the bunny out of her way, Kiara could smell wolf. Their intermingled scents indicated the monster-bunny-bear-thing and wolf were mated to each other.

The scary man gave Sebastian a little shake when he saw where Sebastian's gaze had gone—right to the blonde's naked body.

"Bethany go put on some clothes," the scary man growled. Even in human form he had a scary wolf's growl.

The blonde just stuck her tongue out at him and pranced back into the room she'd come out of; with just her head sticking out the door she smiled at Kiara. "I'm going to bet whatever he did, he totally deserved what he had coming to him, but we weren't sure what was going on. Sorry if I ruined your fun! You're adorable, by the way."

Neither Kiara nor her doe really knew how to react, but the blonde-bunny-monster didn't seem to expect a reaction, since she pulled her head back as soon as she finished speaking and shut the door.

Scary man (who was even taller and more intimidating than Dorian!) looked at Kiara, Sebastian still half-hanging from his hand. Sebastian looked anywhere *but* at her. "So what the fuck is going on and what the hell is she?"

"I'd like the answer to the first question as well." The cool, professional voice of Dr. Tran came from behind Kiara and her herd. Sneaky doctor, she'd moved so quietly, and Kiara had been so engrossed in the big ass bunny she hadn't even heard the woman arriving.

Dorian swung around to face her. Although she'd sounded completely blasé, Dr. Tran's lips still quirked when she caught sight of Kiara hanging from Dorian's side. For a moment Kiara considered shifting... but that would still leave her hanging because Dorian was so darned tall, and with her entire backside presented to Sebastian and the scary dude.

No thanks, she'd pass on that particular humiliation.

Dr. Tran looked past her and fixed Sebastian with a hard gaze. "Mr. Sirrobin, I believe I informed you that Ms. Arrio was on her way and that your concerns would be addressed. I definitely did *not* tell you that you could attempt to make off with her as you attempted to do."

Dorian turned enough that Kiara could see the men behind them. Sebastian's attempt to draw himself back up in front of the diminutive doctor was hampered by the scary guy's refusal to let go of his shirt collar.

"Madam, I simply attempted to approach my mate and reclaim her from these... *men*." His voice dripped with disdain as he looked at Kiara's herd. She bared her teeth at him and he shuddered. Yeah, not so interested in her now, was he?

Jerk.

She couldn't believe she'd ever thought he was her mate.

Actually, yes, she could. She and the other females had been fed a pack of lies.

On the other hand, believing those lies and following the rules had also kept all of them safe. She'd been out in regular shifter society long enough to know that much of the small shifter population had been decimated—some had even gone extinct.

The Pudu deer population might be skewed towards males, but it was also stable, and no one was dying of any awful illnesses. She'd managed to catch one within months of leaving the community.

"Since I'm no longer interested in having her, I believe I'll be on my way," Sebastian said, attempting to pull away from the firm grip on his collar.

If a doe could have snickered, Kiara would have when he got absolutely nowhere.

The door next to them all opened again, and the blonde came back out, her blue eyes sparkling. She smiled sunnily at Kiara, completely ignoring Sebastian.

"Aren't you just the sweetest little doe?! Bailey's going to be so sad she missed seeing you!" Bethany said, bending forward and putting her hands on her knees. Not really sure what to make of her—and very aware of how big the bunny was in comparison to herself—Kiara just looked back at her. Thankfully it wasn't like a response was required. She could feel Dorian chuckling though. He was totally going to pay for that later. "I didn't even know a full-grown doe could be this tiny! And look at your teeth!"

"She's a freak!" Sebastian spat.

"Alright, that's enough," Alec snapped, starting forward. Scary dude gave him a stern look while Gavin grabbed his arm.

"Everybody calm down," Dr. Tran said, stepping into the middle of everyone. "We're *all* going to Eli's office. *Now.*"

On the trip to Eli's office (she was pretty sure he was her herd's boss), the scary dude frog-marched Sebastian in front of him. Kiara was still tucked under Dorian's arm (which, seriously, how was he not getting tired?! She wasn't *that* light, even as a doe!) and the others walked around them. The blonde walked beside Kiara, talking to her the whole way.

"Hi, I'm Bethany. That's my mate, Steele." She cheerfully pointed at the scary dude. "My sister-in-law Jesse told me about you, but she didn't tell me how small you actually are. I was kind of skeptical that deer could be small shifters, but we looked it up on the internet. I bet you were adorable as a baby." She looked around at the men. "Congratulations on the mating... those are some nice bite marks. On all of them too! Thorough. Can't blame you for marking them up, pronto. Nice looking herd you have here."

The growl which went through the hallway wasn't Kiara's—it was Steele's. He shot his mate a look over his shoulder, glowering. "You have more than you can handle with *one* mate, sweetheart."

"Too true," Bethany agreed. She leaned in towards Kiara, lowering her voice even though it wouldn't actually hide any of what she was saying. "He's an awfully grouchy mate. But the sex... totally makes up for it. Still... four males. Do you—"

"*Bethany.*"

Winking at Kiara, Bethany seemed completely pleased to be annoying her large and intimidating mate. Crazy bunny. Although... Kiara peeked up at Dorian just as they came to a halt in front of an office door. Steele knocked on the door with his fist.

As if feeling Kiara's gaze on him, Dorian looked down at her. Raised his eyebrow.

Shook his head.

Don't even think about it, was the silent message she got. Dorian would never tolerate being prodded and purposefully annoyed the way Bethany was doing with Steele.

I bet Bethany's mate doesn't spank her, Kiara thought a little sulkily.

Do it anyway, whispered her doe, not at all bothered by the idea of a spanking, and more than a little amused at the prospect of copying Bethany's outspoken ways.

She had a feeling her doe was going to get her into trouble. If she hadn't already, that was.

******

Eli, it turned out, was definitely the big boss.

As in, *the* big boss. Of all shifters. Unofficially.

Kiara hadn't even known there was such a thing.

Sebastian definitely had though. The minute Eli had been introduced as Eli *Mansfield*, Sebastian had turned a strange pasty white under his tan and had sat down very heavily in the seat. Although the latter might have had a little to do with Steele's hand pushing him down.

Sitting down in the other chair in front of Eli's desk, Dorian kept Kiara cradled on his lap.

All things considered, she honestly was perfectly happy to stay in her doe form right now. Especially because every time Sebastian looked at her, all she had to do was lift her lip a little and flash some fang to make him immediately avert his eyes.

Both she and her doe might be getting off on scaring him.

Just a little.

She could feel amusement wafting through her mind from her four mates as Sebastian glanced at her again. He seemed to be having some difficulty avoiding both Eli's gaze *and* hers without appearing at a disadvantage.

Everyone went through their story, except for Kiara, while Eli listened patiently. The only time he spoke was to congratulate her herd on their mating, his eyes flicking over the marks on their necks with amusement before resting on her for a moment as if contemplating a tiny doe with such sharp teeth. When it was his turn, Sebastian tried to make it sound like he had just been trying to check on her, but he hadn't been able to completely hide his disdain for Dr. Tran's orders or his disgust and fear of Kiara now that he'd seen her shifted doe.

Finally, Eli turned his cool, blue gaze on Kiara. He raised an eyebrow at her. He was gorgeous. Not in the same way Sebastian's good looks were attractive, no, Eli's appeal went far beyond that. Blond hair, blue eyes, firm jawline, but with real charm in his face and kindness. He looked like he smiled more than he frowned, and he gave off a kind of aura of command that made Sebastian and the other elders look like pale imitations of authority.

"So, Kiara. Pleasure to meet you. Would you like to shift to human and join in the conversation now?" He sounded amused, at least, but Kiara still hesitated.

Bethany let out a huffy noise of exasperation. "Really, Eli? In a room full of men, fully clothed and half of them not her mates, you want her to just shift and answer questions naked?"

Groaning, Steele dragged his hand over his face at his mate's disrespectful chiding of the most powerful shifter in the room—possibly in the country, if Kiara had understood everything correctly.

Kiara looked at the other woman in awe. Was there no one who intimidated her? Kiara decided right then and there, when she grew up, she wanted to be Bethany. Yeah, she was already an adult, but she felt like she had a lot of catching up to do when it came to actually *being* a real 'grown-up' in this new world of hers. When she finished growing, being just like Bethany was definitely her end goal.

As if they could sense some of her determination, her herd shifted their own stances a little uneasily.

Eli looked back at Bethany, amusement dancing in his eyes. Apparently, he didn't mind the mouthy bunny shifter—or maybe he was just used to her.

"She's a shifter, Bethany," he said, as if that explained everything.

Bethany rolled her eyes. "I'm a shifter and I don't like getting naked in front of a bunch of men I don't know."

"Don't mind when they get naked in front of you though," her mate said grumpily. The grouchy expression on his face subsided a bit when Bethany grinned and leaned into him, rubbing her face on his chest.

"You still win every comparison," she whispered. Everyone pretended they hadn't heard that.

Sighing, Eli ran his hand through his blond locks and looked back at Kiara. "Ms. Arrio, if we all look away and perhaps one of your stags can provide you with—yes, thank you, Riley. We will all look away and you can shift and put on Riley's shirt in peace so I can speak with you directly, that would be much appreciated."

Soft fabric draped over her back. Eli turned his head, Bethany pulled her mate down for a kiss to make sure his eyes were averted, and Gavin and Alec stepped in between the chair she and Dorian were on and the chair Sebastian was sitting in to make sure he couldn't even try to peek. They were like a big wall of man.

The thought had Kiara grinning as she shifted on Dorian's lap, feeling a little silly there. He and Riley helped her quickly yank Riley's shirt over herself. The hem fell down to about mid-thigh, making her feel even smaller. As soon as she had it on, Dorian's arm curled around her waist, hauling her back to lean against him, his fingers draping over her hip and caressing.

So apparently, she was just supposed to sit on his lap through the interview.

Oh well. There were worse places.

"She's good," Dorian said, his chest rumbling against her back. As Eli opened his eyes again, the rest of the herd arrayed themselves around the chair—Riley to the right with his arms crossed over his bare chest while Alec and Gavin kept their position between her and Sebastian. Since she was feeling a little less brave out of her doe form, she didn't mind their protective stance at all.

"Hello, Ms. Arrio," Eli said, giving her an absolutely devastating smile. If she hadn't already mated her herd, she would have probably melted into a little puddle. Dorian's arm tightened a little around her body. Oops. She'd better watch those thoughts. Her males were definitely *very* good at picking up on her emotions. "It's very nice to finally meet you."

"Hello," she said, her voice soft. Despite wanting to be as ballsy and blunt as Bethany, she found herself now feeling rather tongue-tied.

"So, Ms. Arrio, please tell me in your own words exactly how you came to be here," Eli requested, still smiling. Good lord, the man could probably charm birds out of their nests with just a flash of his white teeth.

She cleared her throat and started to talk. Under Eli's sympathetic gaze, with her herd around her bolstering her confidence, and Steele's heavy hand squeezing Sebastian's shoulder whenever he tried to interrupt, she ended up saying much more than she'd even meant to.

She told them about the Pudu deer community, about the elders matching up the females with their 'mates.' She also told him about getting a job as an editor and her first time reading a human romance, the yearning it had awoken in her, and her dissatisfaction with her mating. That was when Sebastian had first started trying to interrupt, apparently unhappy with her description of their relationship. Dorian cradled her even closer, one of Riley's hands reaching out to play with a lock of her hair as she told Eli about deciding she could no longer live the way she had been and telling Sebastian she no longer wanted to be his mate.

All hell broke loose in the office when she'd mentioned his enraged reaction, which had left her with bruised ribs and a black eye at the time.

Alec was the first to go for Sebastian's throat—and Steele couldn't hold him back because he was too busy holding on to his own mate who was now shrieking with outrage and clawing at the back of Sebastian's chair in her own rage. Kiara had managed to grab Gavin to keep him from doing the same as Alec—and she wasn't sure what Dorian would have done if she weren't literally sitting on him. She could feel him shaking with suppressed rage beneath her, his arms holding her very tightly now. Three of the bundles of emotion in her head had gone hot with anger... one was very cold, ice cold.

A glance over her shoulder gave her a glimpse of Riley's expression, which was completely blank and scary as all heck. Kiara suddenly had the suspicion that he was actually the most dangerous out of all her mates, which explained why he'd been leading the way into the hospital with Dorian. She'd kind of wondered about that, because he came off as the least intimidating at first glance.

Now his gaze was hyper-focused on the tiny male Pudu deer shivering on the other side of the empty chair.

"That's not fair!" Alec roared in frustration, straightening up from where he'd practically thrown himself over the seat of Sebastian's chair. He glared at the small male deer. "How am I supposed to kick his ass when he's a fourth of the size of me?"

"I'll do it!" Bethany shrieked from where Steele was literally holding her off the ground in his arms. She twisted, struggling against her mate's strong arms, trying to kick him. "I don't care how small he is, I'll squash him like a bug!"

Considering she could do that just by turning into her monster-bunny and sitting on him, it was a pretty valid threat. In Kiara's head, she could hear her doe snickering.

Eli stood up, drawing everyone's attention to him, and the stony look on his face had washed away all his charm. The aura of innate power around him practically pulsed and Kiara suddenly found it hard to breathe as her doe quivered in

Kiara's head, rolling on her back to show her submission to the Alpha. Blue eyes alight with anger, he gave everyone a quelling look, which had immediate effect. Bethany sagged in her mate's arms, no longer struggling to free herself and get at Sebastian, and Alec allowed himself to be pulled closer to Kiara. She grabbed hold of his hand with one of hers, and Riley's with the other. Gavin seemed to have himself under control now, although he'd still shifted his stance to ensure Sebastian's tiny deer couldn't get anywhere near her.

Turning his gaze to Sebastian, Eli's expression became supremely disdainful. "Mr. Sirrobin, I suggest you stay in that form as Ms. Arrio's mates are too honorable to attack someone smaller and physically weaker than themselves. You might take a lesson from that. Also, stay away from Bethany if you want to live. If you're too stupid to do so, I'll consider it Darwinism." He turned back to Kiara as he sat down. "Please continue, Ms. Arrio."

Still a little bemused by everyone's reactions—Kiara finished her story. Although, of course, her herd knew most of it. The entire time Sebastian stayed cowered next to the wall, both eyes on Bethany, who was glaring back at him. She wasn't even sure Sebastian was listening to a word she was saying. Which was fine by her.

When she finished, Eli nodded his head solemnly.

"Thank you, Ms. Arrio. I think it's clear you're where you're meant to be." He smiled briefly at her before turning a much less friendly gaze onto Sebastian's still-quivering buck. "If you would all excuse us, I think Mr. Sirrobin and I have quite a bit to discuss."

Chapter 9

"Damnit," Bethany said, pouting and staring at Eli's closed door. "I wanted to see Eli eat him."

"He's not going to eat him," Steele said, sounding exasperated as he glared down at his mate. Kiara couldn't help but watch the two of them in fascination. He was so huge and intimidating, and at first glance she was so petite and delicate she was incredibly easy to underestimate. "He's not nearly as blood-thirsty as you are."

Making a face of disappointment, Bethany sighed. "You're probably right. Too bad though, he sounds like he deserves it."

Turning around, Bethany caught Kiara's gaze and smiled widely at her, coming forward to take her hand, which Kiara immediately offered up. "It really is great to meet you. Now I'm doubly sorry I got in your way earlier. If I'd known, I would have made sure you caught that... pretentious assbutt!"

"Assbutt?" Alec asked, saying the insult slowly as if testing out how it tasted on his tongue.

Steele sighed again. "She's been catching up on pop culture and we hit the Supernatural stage about a month ago."

"What's Supernatural?" Kiara asked.

Immediately, Bethany's eyes lit up and all five men groaned in unison.

******

After dinner with Steele and Bethany—during which Alec definitely won the most brownie points with his new interest in Supernatural (what? 'Assbutt' was a great insult. His new interest was legitimate.)—the men all piled back into the car with Kiara to head back to the cabin. They might only have two more days left in their vacation, but they were determined to make the most of them.

Before dinner Dorian had made sure to request a new rooming situation for them on base, now that they had a mate. Kiara's job meant she could work anywhere and she seemed relieved to stay at Lakewood. Especially after Bethany told her that she, Jesse, and Bethany's sister Bailey often swung by for visits with her brother Brice, who was currently part of the teams hunting down The Company's research sites. Not the same team Alec and the others were currently on but doing the same work.

He was still pissed as all hell about what his poor mate had been through, prior to running away. His stag was chafing to give Sebastian a good spiking with his antlers. Although Alec was really glad she *had* run away. But he still wished he'd been able to get at least one good punch in before the assbutt had shifted into such a small, helpless deer that Alec couldn't even feel good about kicking him.

During the drive home Kiara asked them a lot more questions about The Company, Bethany Bunson and her siblings, and their duties at Lakewood. It wasn't surprising that her interest had been piqued. After all, as far as Alec knew, Jesse and her brother and the Bunson family were the only other beneficiaries of Dr. Montgomery's work. On the other hand, there might be others. Eli was doing his best to keep Kiara's identity under wraps, at least until the Walkers and Kiara were back at Lakewood.

Safety in secrecy.

She also wanted to know what they thought Eli might have wanted to discuss with Sebastian, but none of them could really hazard a guess.

Well, they were all pretty sure Eli probably had something to say about Kiara's treatment at Sebastian's hands, but after that it was anyone's guess. Personally, Alec was going to be pretty mad if Sebastian got away with nothing but a stern talking-to. That didn't really seem Eli's style though. They would just have to wait and see.

When they all got back into the main room of the cabin, Kiara stood in the center of the room and looked around. They all looked back at her, waiting to see what she wanted to do. Alec knew what *he* wanted to do, but he didn't know what kind of mood she was in after confronting her ex and then dinner with one of the loudest and noisiest people he'd ever met—Bethany, obviously, not Steele.

Turning back to them, Kiara yawned.

Stretched.

The movement tugged the hem of her shirt up—she was still wearing Riley's shirt—and it was just long enough to cover everything they really wanted to see. But all three of them watched the hem travel upwards, revealing another inch or so of thigh, hoping it would go just a little bit farther.

"Oh!" she said, delicately putting her hand over her mouth, eyelashes fluttering at them mischievously. "I'm *so* tired. I think maybe I should go to bed early."

Alec jumped forward ahead of the rest of them—too slow, too bad, suckers!—and scooped his giggling mate up in his arms. She wound her arms around his neck as he headed straight for the stairs. "Early to bed sounds good, let me just make sure you get there okay... wouldn't want you falling asleep on the stairs... in the hall..."

He didn't even need to look over his shoulder to see the rest of the men following behind him.

Our mate. The prominent emotion coming off of his stag was satisfied smugness. *Good mate.*

Yeah, she definitely was an amazing mate. Gorgeous, smart, sassy, and one of the strongest people Alec had ever met—and he'd thought so even before he'd heard the full story.

"I think I should ensure I get my shirt back," Riley said casually, following Alec and Kiara into her room. Giggling even harder, Kiara peeked over Alec's shoulder at him, and then let out a little shriek of delight as Alec tossed her onto the bed and crawled on after her with Riley right behind him. Alec's cock was already at full mast, ready to be buried inside of her.

"This shirt?" Alec asked, pushing it up above her breasts, exposing her body to him.

"Yes, I'm definitely going to need that back," Riley said matter-of-factly, making Alec grin. It wasn't often his brother was playful, but apparently Kiara brought it out in him.

Together they pulled it over Kiara's head and she fell back down on the bed on her back, stretching her arms up and thrusting her breasts at them. It almost succeeded in looking like a completely innocent, casual movement.

Lowering his mouth down, Alec sucked the pert nipple closest to him into his mouth, while across her body his brother was doing the same thing. The tiny bud was stiff and swollen against his tongue as he suckled, and her moan as she slid her hand into his hair made his dick throb with need.

******

Oh have mercy… that felt amazing!

Both men were nibbling and sucking at her nipples with their own special flair, making her ache between her thighs as the incredible double sensation sent electricity sizzling through her. Kiara writhed between them, pressing her thighs together as need swamped her.

She and her doe were practically panting with the need for them. Any thoughts she'd had about her libido dying down once they were mated had pretty much disappeared. After their protectiveness with Sebastian, the dinner with Bethany and Steele (which they had obviously only agreed to because she'd wanted it), the long car-ride where they'd patiently answered every single one of her questions as thoroughly as possible, Kiara had never felt so loved, so cared-for.

They were doing everything for her.

It was the ultimate aphrodisiac as far as she was concerned.

Although, having her nipples simultaneously sucked was definitely pretty far up there on the list of things that really turned her on, too.

"Flip her over," Gavin suddenly said from just above her head. Kiara opened her eyes and looked up to see him kneeling there, already naked and hand wrapped around his cock, pumping its thick length as he watched her writhing before him with hot eyes.

She mewled in disappointment as the hot suction on her nipples ceased and she was flipped onto all fours. On the other hand, her doe liked this position a lot.

Arching her back to lift her bottom further in the air, she shivered as Gavin's fingers slid into her hair, using his grip to draw her lips to his cock. Opening her mouth, Kiara lapped her tongue around the fat head of his dick. Groaning, his fingers tightened in her hair as she sucked him in deeper, tasting the sweet-salt of his pre-cum. So many hands were running over her body, her sides, her breasts, her thighs, she couldn't possibly keep track of whose were whose even if she tried.

When two of them gripped onto her bottom cheeks, spreading them, she didn't immediately realize why until she felt something wet and cool press against her anus. It felt shocking and delicious at the same time, and she moaned as a finger swirled around the little bud then began to press in.

Oh goodness… that felt…

Wicked. Depraved. Sinful. And oh, so good.

Kiara whined around Gavin's cock as the finger thrust, burrowing deeper inside of her most intimate area. It felt so strange, but pleasurable too, and both she and her doe were fascinated by the new sensations being stirred up by the intrusion.

"Fuck… I think she likes it, Dorian…" Gavin said, his voice a growl as he moved his hips, the head of his cock bumping against the back of her throat as she hummed her enjoyment around his shaft. She did like it. She liked the full feeling, the perversity and unexpectedness of it, and how incredibly intimate it felt.

No one else had ever touched her there before.

The finger withdrew and was almost immediately replaced by something harder, something slicker. She gasped around Gavin's cock as it pushed into her, stretching her tiny hole. The hands on her breasts squeezed and tugged, pinching at her nipples and distracting her from the sharp burn of her muscles opening.

There was a quick, sharp cramp as it pushed in deeper, stretching her wide... and then the worst of the sting was past and there was something inside of her, holding her open. It felt even odder. Especially when whoever had inserted it—she suspected Dorian—tugged on it, pulling it against her tight muscle from the other side.

"Oh she definitely likes it," Dorian said with satisfaction, confirming her theory. Fingers trailed over the lips of her swollen pussy, which was hot and wet. She moaned around Gavin's thrusting cock, pushing up to try for more stimulation. "She's soaked."

As if by some secret signal—the males were probably doing one of those silent conversations with their eyes again—Dorian and Alec suddenly moved, switching places. Kiara gasped, Gavin's cock pushing into her throat as Alec thrust forward into her pussy.

Whatever Dorian had filled her ass with made her feel incredibly tight, as if there was barely enough room for Alec inside of her as well. Her fingers dug into the bed beneath her as Alec's hands gripped her hips and he began to thrust, pushing her back and forth on his and Gavin's cocks, while Riley slid beneath her and began his meticulously sensual assault on her breasts.

She was drowning in sensation and she never wanted it to stop.

******

Kiara's moans and whimpers as Alec fucked her were sending incredible vibrations up the length of Gavin's cock, making his spine tingle as he matched his movements to Alec's. Looking down at their pretty mate, her pink lips wrapped around the slick length of his cock, he could see the expression of extreme pleasure on her face. Her eager suckling was as arousing as it was pleasurable. She was sucking him like she couldn't get enough of him, like she couldn't take him deep enough into her mouth.

Every thrust of Alec's cock into her pussy pushed her forward on Gavin's cock, her tongue dancing along the underside, driving him wild. With his hand in her hair, he was able to help hold her up, keeping her steady as she was rocked between them, a willing toy to their pleasure.

Dorian watched from the side of them, his eyes glued to where Kiara was swallowing Gavin's cock. The twins always got off on watching each other, because it was like watching himself—as long as he didn't look at his brother's face. Although, Gavin had to say, he liked the view he had better than the one Dorian did.

As their mate's pleasure-filled gaze lifted to meet his eyes, Gavin shuddered. He could feel his balls tightening as he tried to hold back his own orgasm, wanting to continue enjoying the hot pleasure of her mouth.

Across from him, Alec was clenching his jaw as he pounded into Kiara from behind, his own orgasm obviously rising and taking hers along with it. Her throat quivered around his cock, and he groaned, fingers pulling her hair tighter as she sucked him harder, deeper, half-choking on his cock in her frenzy to swallow him.

"Oh fuck..." Gavin threw his head back as she sucked harder, her mouth growing more frantic as her own pleasure climbed higher.

He thrust forward and held himself still in the hot, wet suction of her mouth, panting for breath as he came. The muscles of her throat worked, milking him of every drop.

******

The lack of air as Gavin's cock moved in and out of Kiara's mouth had made her dizzy, and yet somehow that only increased her pleasure. She was riding a wave of erotic rapture, so wonderfully full, so incredibly overcome with every man's touch on her body.

Riley's mouth was moving back and forth between her nipples, his hands and fingers kneading and pinching, the never-ceasing stimulation driving her absolutely wild.

As Gavin finally came, she felt a surge of savage satisfaction as he poured his pleasure down her throat, accompanied by her own body's clenching as her passion spiraled higher. Her bottom was clenching around whatever Dorian had filled it with, giving her an entirely new avenue of pleasure as Alec's hard thrusts against the base of it made it feel almost as though it was pushing deeper every time he did.

The sweet taste of Gavin's cream was on her tongue as he pulled from her mouth, leaving her only focus on Alec pumping in and out of her pussy. Without Gavin to work his movements with, Alec could ride her as hard as he liked, to his own rough rhythm. Her nipples throbbed, her pussy spasmed, and she screamed as Alec's hard thrusts sent her over the edge. His balls slapped against her swollen clit, sending orgasmic ecstasy in hot waves through her body.

She barely noticed as Riley's mouth pulled away from her nipples, his hands still plumping her breasts as she shook and moaned through her climax. Alec's cock throbbed against her clenching sheath. Gripping her tightly, he buried himself completely inside of her with an ecstatic shout announcing his own completion.

******

"Good girl," Dorian murmured to their quivering mate, his hands sliding down her sides as he and Alec switched places. Alec took up position on the opposite side of Riley, caressing her, murmuring his own compliments, as Gavin stroked her hair and neck.

"You're so beautiful."

"So incredible."

"So perfect."

She shivered as Dorian laid kisses down across her lower back, idly playing with the base of the plug he'd inserted to stretch out her ass for him. Every time he twisted it, she reacted with excited arousal.

"I love you…" She gasped out the words, practically burying her face in the mattress as if she couldn't hold the declaration back any longer but wanted to hide from the vulnerability it created.

Good mate.

The smug thought from his stag made Dorian smile as he added his own declaration to the others.

"We love you, Kiara."

"We love you."

"We all love you, lovely girl."

"You're ours now, good girl. Forever and always." Almost reverently, Dorian smoothed his hands over her upturned backside as he spoke.

She was everything any of them could have asked for and he still couldn't quite believe how lucky they were. Looking around at the rest of their faces—well, everyone's except Riley since he was still underneath Kiara, playing with her breasts—Dorian knew they felt the same. And he didn't need to see Riley's expression to know he was on the same wavelength.

Gavin slid down onto his side so he could start kissing Kiara, his fingers still in her hair, as Alec stroked and caressed her back. They knew exactly what Dorian wanted to do to her and they all came together to make it as easy and enjoyable as possible.

Their pretty mate moaned against Gavin's lips as Dorian pumped the plug, stretching the tight entrance of her ass using the widest part of the toy. She didn't object at all. If anything, her arousal increased, her body moving in time with the toy's shallow strokes.

✶✶✶✶✶✶

The toy slid out, leaving Kiara feeling empty and needy. The sensations had been so different but so good. She whimpered into Gavin's mouth, kissing him more deeply as Riley continued to lavish attention on her breasts, Alec's hands stroking her back.

Then Dorian's hands gripped her hips, his cock pressing against the tight opening he'd just been using the toy to play with, and she cried out at the shockingly intimate sensation of his slick cock pushing into her virgin hole. He'd obviously spread some kind of lubricant all over his length, because her clenching muscles couldn't actually grip him at all. The burn of discomfort as he slid deeper made her ache all through her core... and yet she didn't want him to stop either.

The other men's hands and lips distracted her from the sting, the small cramps as Dorian rocked back and forth, pushing himself a little deeper with each thrust. Kiara had never felt so submissive. Even her doe was quietly meek inside of her, wanting to give the stags everything they desired from her. When Dorian finally came to rest, fully sheathed inside of her, she thought she might explode from the arousal and need coursing through her.

She felt so deliciously full, so sensuously invaded, so perfectly consumed by her love for the four men all intensely focused on her.

The slide of Dorian's cock out of her and then back in had her crying out, the sound muffled by Gavin's kiss as Alec's hands stroked down her back, massaging. Her breasts throbbed in Riley's hands as Dorian moved, stimulating all sorts of nerve endings and making her feel utterly wild.

He began moving a little faster, a little more easily, and the drag and glide of his cock felt perversely sensual. She felt her entire body shaking at the intimate stimulation, the strange burn it created inside of her, and when he suddenly pulled out, she cried out in disappointment.

******

The wild look in Kiara's eyes as Riley pulled her atop him was indescribable. She was sensuality incarnate, overtaken with erotic abandon. His cock was aching, dying to be inside of her.

Her breasts heaved above him as Dorian helped her straddle Riley's hips. The swollen mounds were plump and pink from his attentions, her nipples swollen and colored a dark, burnished red from all his pinching and sucking. Whimpering, she slid down onto his cock easily, her pussy slick and hungry to be filled.

Riley groaned, lifting his hips up to meet hers. He was tangentially aware of Gavin and Alec sitting back and watching, enjoying seeing their mate take her pleasure between two of them.

The moment she was seated atop him, Kiara began to move, obviously anxious for her pleasure. He enjoyed two good bounces of her sweet pussy on his cock before Dorian's hands caught her hips again and she stilled. Her needy moan of disappointment made Riley's cock pulse.

"Hold still, lovely," he said. "Just give Dorian a moment."

Her eyes widened and then lit with shock and pleasure as Dorian began to slide back into her ass. Riley could feel the thick length pushing into her body, separated from his by the thin lining of her inner walls.

"Oh goodness... oh... oh, I can't... oh God..." Kiara writhed as Dorian filled her. Despite her words, Riley could tell she was in no distress.

The opposite in fact.

She was on the verge of feeling so much pleasure, she could barely tolerate it.

And they were about to make her feel even better.

"That's it, good girl," Dorian said huskily, his voice strained as he bottomed out. Now they were both fully inside of Kiara and she was quivering between them like a harp-string about to snap. "Fuck you feel so good..."

"I... I... Oh!" She gasped as Riley rocked his hips, unable to remain completely still, and her body clenched down on both of them.

"Gorgeous," Riley murmured, lifting his hands back up to her breasts. She whimpered, looking down at him, her eyes hazy with lust and pleasure. "You are perfection."

He felt Dorian began to recede and pulled his own hips back when his cousin began to thrust back in, working their bodies in tandem to drive her to the highest heights of ecstasy. Between them, Kiara writhed at the new sensations, and part of Riley's brain obsessively catalogued every single one of her reactions for future reference even as his own ecstasy grew.

******

Full? She hadn't known what the word meant.

Now she did. She was crammed, packed to bursting, her lower body absolutely crowded with hard cock.

Was there such a thing as excessive pleasure?

Because she felt like she'd hit that and gone beyond.

Every movement Riley and Dorian made was exquisite torment, sending her higher on a plane of sensation that she hadn't even known existed.

Practically sobbing between them, she could feel Gavin and Alec's eyes on her, their voyeurism only adding to her excitement, enhancing her pleasure in the proceedings.

"Oh yes..."

Riley and Dorian moved in conjunction with each other. Riley slid inside of her as Dorian pulled away, then Dorian pushed back inside of her, rocking her off of Riley's cock. Each surge sent her spiraling. Her body clenched, trying to hold them still because she couldn't possibly handle the onslaught, and yet if they stopped she would use her doe's fangs and bite them as viciously as she could.

Her entrances were slick and fully stretched for them, and the men moved faster, harder. Their cocks jostling for space inside of her, making her feel crazed with pleasure and turning her into a creature of pure erotic demand.

"Oh yes please..."

Alec and Gavin moved in closer, unable to stay away, their hands touching her... she was surrounded by her mates. They were inside of her, all over her, and she screamed her bliss as she came, tumbling into an orgasm so intense she blacked out.

******

When Kiara awoke later, she had very vague, muzzy memories of being taken to the shower and gently washed off by one of her mates while she slumped against another who held her up. She couldn't even remember which of her males had been in the shower with her.

Every part of her body felt sensitive and sore in the best way possible.

Opening her eyes, she looked around in the darkness. It occurred to her that she definitely saw even better in the darkness than she used to. Her doe purred in acknowledgment.

Propping herself up on her elbows, she turned her head back and forth, and smiled.

All four men were in bed with her, fast asleep. Dorian was on the outside closest to the door with Gavin beside him, twinned hotness. On her other side, Alec was cuddled up to her with his and Riley's backs touching.

This was not what she had ever expected, not the life she'd ever seen for herself or even dreamed to hope for.

It was so much better.

Epilogue

Watching the Pudu deer shifters lining up to receive their gamut of vaccines, Kiara felt an overwhelming sense of satisfaction.

Unfortunately, the vaccines wouldn't do anything for smaller shifters who had already been infected by the diseases, but for the first time there was real hope for those small shifter populations who were left. Changing DNA, like had been done for Kiara, wasn't exactly a viable solution for everyone—especially since smaller shifters tended be insular even before diseases had started to strike them harder than the larger shifters. It had been pure luck Kiara had a larger shifter in her ancestry and could be cured of the Scourge using Dr. Montgomery's treatment.

However, for her old community, it was going to make a world of difference. They'd been living in two large apartment buildings just on the outskirts of a small, completely human town, with not another shifter around for miles. For smaller shifters intent on isolating themselves and ensuring they didn't contract any of the shifter diseases which were deadly to them, it was actually a really perfect setup.

It just hadn't been the right life for her, and probably not for some of the others either.

The other deer would no longer have to be sequestered in these buildings, unless they wanted to be. Many of them (especially the older ones) had already indicated they would be staying, but there were also quite a few who seemed thrilled at the chance to leave. More than one of those were now eyeing some of the male Lakewood hospital workers and the few soldiers who had come to help with the process.

Several of the male Pudu were looking a little disgruntled, but even there the reactions seemed to be split down the middle. A few of them even looked a little relieved, especially two younger males who were hovering over the same female. All three of *them* kept looking over at Kiara and her herd with wide, contemplative gazes.

Seeing Elder Maynard approaching her, his five mates following obediently along behind him, Kiara drew herself up to face him. He was the oldest and most respected Elder.

As he drew closer, her own herd shifted around her like a coterie of bodyguards. Dorian and Riley were in front of her, of course, and Gavin and Alec beside and just behind her. Stopping a few feet away, Elder Maynard gave them all respectful nods, his wrinkled face calm and composed, before focusing on Kiara.

Now that he and his mates were so close, she was startled to realize that their scents did indeed overlap, the same way hers did with her mates. She supposed she'd always thought it was from long association with each other, but now she knew he actually had mated with each and every one of them, just as she had with her herd. It made her feel a little better to know for sure that not all of the matings of her community had been as empty as hers to Sebastian.

"Kiara, it's good to see you again," Elder Maynard said in his quavering, croaky voice, sounding perfectly sincere. His white eyebrows quivered as he frowned in regret. "I would like to extend my deepest apologies to you. We had no idea your mating to Sebastian was so unsatisfactory or that he would ever be violent. Mr. Mansfield tells me he is to be prosecuted, which is quite a relief."

Since Kiara had never expected Sebastian would be either, she couldn't exactly fault Elder Maynard. Nor did she blame him for being relieved that Sebastian wouldn't be his problem. As influential as Sebastian had been in the community, it was probably for the best that Eli was taking care of Sebastian himself.

"It's alright, Elder," she said, smiling and ignoring her males' grumbles around her. They weren't going to be as quick to forgive her old community, she could tell. "It turned out for the best."

Not unexpectedly, the grumbling cut off and suddenly all four males were radiating smug happiness. Kiara didn't bother to hide her grin.

"I can see that," Elder Maynard said, his eyes crinkling as he smiled at her. "Congratulations on your mating. I'm sure this one will be much more successful."

"Me too," she said, beaming back at him.

Nodding, he moved on, his mates following behind him, perfectly content to just go where he did.

It would be interesting to see which deer decided to leave the compound and which stayed, Kiara mused. Looking across the field to where her own mother was standing in line to receive her vaccination, she had a feeling she knew of at least one deer who would be staying. Her mother had deigned to be introduced to Kiara's mates, but she hadn't been especially interested and she had shown no desire for anything in her own little world to change.

Which was fine. Kiara was sad her mother couldn't be different, but she didn't feel an empty void inside of her anymore, or an ache to be touched and loved. Not only did she have her mates, but she had a whole new life at Lakewood, where she was already making friends.

"Do you think maybe they were part of the impetus to move towards multiple females with one male as the norm?" Riley asked, watching the retreating Elder Maynard and his herd. "Obviously it happened in conjunction with the declining male population, but—"

Alec groaned, cutting his brother off. "Dude, just don't even start. Please."

Giggling, Kiara slipped her arm around Riley's waist. "I think that probably had something to do with it. Obviously they made it successful even if not everyone did."

Claiming her other side, his arm around her shoulders, Gavin smiled down at her. "So you're good?"

Looking around at all her brethren, knowing a whole new world was about to open for any who wanted it, Kiara smiled at each of her mates in turn. Dorian, who was still standing slightly in front of her watching for any threat. Alec, who looked like he was contemplating trying to push either Gavin or Riley out of his way and take one of the spots at her side. Gavin with his protectiveness and silly behavior, and sweet Riley with his constant questions and hidden depths.

Good?

That word didn't even begin to encompass what she was feeling.

"I'm outstanding," she said.

Turning slightly, Dorian's lips curved up as he caught her eye. "That you are, love."

Grinning, she leaned her head against Gavin's shoulder as she continued watching the other Pudu deer talk and joke and flirt with outside shifters for the first time in years.

It was a new era for the small shifters and her community.

Kiara hoped they all got their own happily-ever-afters, just like she had.

About the Author

About me? Right... I'm a writer, I should be able to do that, right?

I'm a happily married young woman, no kids so far, and I like tater tots, small fuzzy animals, naming my plants, hiking, reading, writing, sexy time, naked time, shirtless o'clock, anything sparkly or shiny, and weirding people out with my OCD food habits.

I believe in Happy Endings. And fairies. And Santa Claus. Because without a little magic, what's the point of living?

I write because I must. I live in several different worlds at any given moment. And I wouldn't have it any other way.

Thank you so much for reading, I hope you enjoyed the story... and don't forget, the best thing you can do in return for any author is to leave them feedback!

Stay sassy.

Made in the USA
Las Vegas, NV
04 March 2025